# JUST KEEP WALKING

## ERIN SODERBERG DOWNING

SCHOLASTIC INC.

Copyright © 2024 by Erin Soderberg Downing

This book is being published simultaneously in hardcover
by Scholastic Press.

All rights reserved. Published by Scholastic Inc., *Publishers since 1920*.
SCHOLASTIC, and associated logos are trademarks and/or registered
trademarks of Scholastic Inc.

Use of the registered trademark "Superior Hiking Trail" name has
been permitted by the Superior Hiking Trail Association.

The publisher does not have any control over and does not assume
any responsibility for author or third-party websites or their content.

No part of this publication may be reproduced, stored in a retrieval
system, or transmitted in any form or by any means, electronic,
mechanical, photocopying, recording, or otherwise, without written
permission of the publisher. For information regarding permission,
write to Scholastic Inc., Attention: Permissions Department, 557
Broadway, New York, NY 10012.

This book is a work of fiction. Names, characters, places, and incidents
are either the product of the author's imagination or are used ficti-
tiously, and any resemblance to actual persons, living or dead,
business establishments, events, or locales is entirely coincidental.

Library of Congress Cataloging-in-Publication Data available

ISBN 978-1-338-85139-7

10 9 8 7 6 5 4 3 2 1          24 25 26 27 28

Printed in the U.S.A.          40

First printing 2024

Book design by Christopher Stengel

Photo © Shutterstock.com

FOR HENRY, OF COURSE.
THANKS FOR STICKING IT OUT (AND KEEPING
ME LAUGHING) FOR A FULL 100 MILES.

CANADA

*Area of detail*

UNITED STATES

PACIFIC
OCEAN

GULF OF MEXICO

ATLANTIC
OCEAN

MINNESOTA

George Crosby
Manitou
State Park

Section 13

Tettegouche
State Park

*Bear
Lake*

Gooseberry Falls
State Park

Silver
Bay

Castle
Danger

*Split Rock River*

L A K E

*St. Louis River*

Duluth

Superior

Jay Cooke
State Park

WISCONSIN

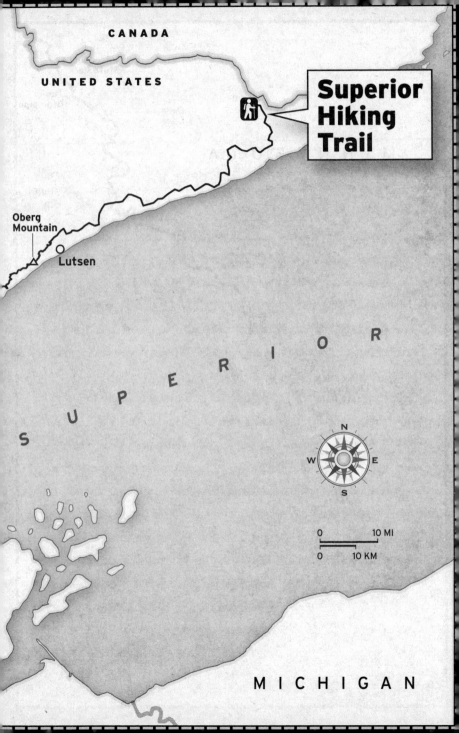

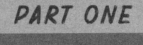

# PART ONE

## CASTLE DANGER

TO

## BEAR LAKE

(39 MILES)

MINNESOTA

Sta

Bear
Lake

Split Rock River

Split Rock
Lighthouse
State Park

erry Falls
tate Park

SUPERIO

---

# CHAPTER ONE
# JUST KEEP WALKING

The toe of my shoe catches a gnarled tree root, my foot twists, and I quickly jab the tip of a hiking pole into the soft dirt at the edge of the path to stop myself from falling. I take another timid step, testing my ankle on the rugged earth.

Sore, not sprained.

Hurt, not broken.

*Just keep walking*, I tell myself.

I limp on, keeping my eyes on the trail, trying to hold back the tears that are already brimming. I promised myself I wouldn't cry. Especially not on the first day of our hike. And certainly not after what Mom told me a few days ago, when we were pulling the tags and packaging off the last of our new gear. "I need to warn you," she'd said, her smile just a weird, wiggly line that made her look like a *Peanuts* character. "I *will* cry when we're out on the trail. Possibly every day."

"Nope, I'm not okay with that," I'd said, shaking my head. "I shouldn't have to deal with a parent crying in front of me. That's not normal."

Mom had laughed, thinking I was being cute. But funny tone or not, I hope she realized I was totally serious. It's awkward to see a parent cry. Wrong. More importantly, if Mom's planning to cry on our hike, that means I can't.

"I don't expect you to *do* anything about it, Jo," Mom had added. "Maybe you can just rub my back or give me a hug, sometimes. And try to remember that I do *want* to be out there with you. I'm the one who offered to do this hike, so that you'd still get to have your big adventure. I just know I'm going to get overwhelmed. This whole thing is a lot." She'd looked at me seriously. "But even if I start crying, it doesn't mean I want to quit. I need you to remember that, since I can't promise that I will."

I try to remember that now, but it doesn't seem fair. *Someone* in our party of two needs to keep it together. But with each step, my ankle feels like someone is jabbing it with a hot poker. Maybe I should have gotten hiking *boots*, instead of quick-drying trail *shoes*, but it's a little late for any *shoulda-woulda-couldas*. I pause, shift my body weight to my hiking poles, roll my foot around in the air, and remind myself to step more carefully from now on. There are going to be a gajillion bumps and roots and rocks ahead, and I'm going to have to figure out how to avoid them.

*Just keep walking.*

The trail slopes up suddenly, a sharp climb to what the Superior Hiking Trail guidebook promises will be a "rewarding view." My pack pinches my shoulders. The skin on my neck stings. There are thirty pounds of food, gear, and my entire life-for-two-weeks crammed into the turtle shell house I'm carrying on my back. Inside the pack, there is a sleeping bag and a thin blow-up sleep pad, the poles for our two-person tent (Mom took the tent and rain fly in her own pack, arguing that because she's bigger, she should lug the extra weight), five dehydrated packaged dinners Mom has promised will be both delicious and nutritious, a tiny folding camp chair, one change of clothes, rain gear, my brother's Swiss Army knife, three water bottles, and a single paperback book that needs to last until we pick up our first food and gear resupply box five days and nearly fifty miles up the trail.

I chose *The Hobbit*.

Because just like Bilbo, I'm setting out on a quest. But unlike Bilbo, mine's not an *unexpected* journey. In fact, I helped plan this adventure. Our trek wasn't sprung on me by a wizard and a pack of dwarves; I *chose* to be here. But as I look ahead at the endless trail of rocks and roots that keeps climbing upward, like a never-ending mountain that's been plopped smack dab in the middle of mostly flat Minnesota, I can't help but wonder: *Why?*

"You holding up okay?" Mom asks, her breath ragged from the climb. "Do you want to lead for a while?"

"No, you can," I tell her. "If I go in front, we're not going to get anywhere fast."

"It's not a race," Mom says. "Want me to walk slower? We have all day."

"This is fine." In time, I'm sure we'll figure out the right speed, who's a better leader and who likes to lag behind, which of us needs a break halfway up each hill and who only stops to rest once they reach the top. My older brother, Jake, told me that's what happened when he and Dad took this same trip together eight years ago. *You have almost two weeks to sort out the kinks*, Jake said with a shrug when I asked him for advice. Just under two weeks, just over one hundred miles. Just a *little* farther up the trail than Dad and Jake made it . . . in part, to annoy Dad. In part, to prove we can.

My feet hurt.

My neck stings.

My legs burn.

I already want to quit. But we're going to finish. If we don't, Dad wins. He's already taken enough from us, and I refuse to let him win by thinking we need him around to lead us through stuff like this. Mom's better off without him, and so am I.

We can do this on our own.

We'll survive, just the two of us.

Dad's a quitter. Not us.

Mom and I walk in silence for a few more minutes, listening to the rustle of birch leaves in the trees overhead. For the past few weeks, I've secretly wondered if we would be stuck chatting about nothing all day—neither Mom nor I do well with awkward silence—or if we'd figure out how to settle into a comfortable quiet. Our house has been a lot quieter lately, especially in those rare times when Mom's gone and I'm home alone. I never used to mind being home by myself; I even sometimes *liked* the space and quiet and responsibility of taking care of myself. But that was before.

Before Jake went back to college, and before Dad side-stepped into his new family.

After, there are way too many uncomfortable silences. Too much time to think about the way things used to be. Too much space to notice the holes in our life. Too many chances to wonder what else might break.

Now alone terrifies me.

*Just keep walking.*

Something shrill screams from the top of a tree just off the trail. I know that sound—a squirrel yelling at us for barging in on its turf and demanding a peace-food offering. I wave up into the trees, trying to be friendly. The squirrel yells again, warning me to move along or pay up. It's not like a squirrel poses much of a threat to us, but there are plenty of other dangers out here: bears, moose, wolves, ticks, poison ivy, dehydration, heat, cold, injuries. I try not to think about those things. But as we settle into our silence, there's too much room to think about everything that scares me.

We come around a corner, and the wall of trees to our left is split open by an enormous boulder jutting out into open sky. I lean against my poles and peer out at the view. It's a sea of green: lime, pine, and emerald all mixed into a water-color canvas of trees that stretches out below us for miles. "That view *is* pretty rewarding," I grumble.

"Oof, I'm pooped already," Mom admits, laughing as she grabs her water bottle out of the side pocket of her pack and takes a long swig. "How far do you think we've gone?"

We set out from the parking lot about an hour ago, probably. We got a lift to the trailhead from one of Mom's friends early this morning. Regina dropped us and our packs at the edge of a gravel parking lot, took a couple quick pictures of us standing together next to the Castle Danger trailhead sign, and cheered as we set off on our merry way. "Maybe two miles?" I guess. We have ten miles planned for today. Ten again tomorrow. Same for the next day. I try not to think about the days of more miles after that, since it gets a little overwhelming when you stack them all up in a line.

Mom pulls out her cell phone, which is set to airplane mode to save the battery, and opens the app she's using to track and map our route for the hike. She glances at the tracker and draws in a breath.

"I don't like your cringe face right now," I say, wiping my forehead. It's only nine in the morning, but it's so hot that a rivulet of sweat has already run down my temple and pooled in my ear. "What's the deal? How far have we gone?"

Mom says nothing.

"Is it *less* than two miles?"

She won't look me in the eye when she says, "Point six."

"Point six what?" I ask. "What does that mean?"

"Six tenths of a mile," she says. "Point six. We've gone just over half a mile. That's it."

"Are you kidding me?" I lift my eyebrows. "This is what half a mile feels like?"

Mom laughs, but it's more of a choked gurgle.

"If this is what *half* a mile feels like," I say, "I'm gonna need to start working on my will right now, because I'm definitely going to die out here." Even though I'm kind of joking, the look on Mom's face tells me this comment isn't very helpful. It's *maybe* not the right attitude to get us through day one. "Come on, we've got this," I say, gently poking her in the butt with the tip of one of my hiking poles. "Let's just keep walking."

# CHAPTER TWO
# CHEWED UP BY A BEAVER

By the time we reach our stopping point for the night, I want to rip my feet right off my body and dump them in the garbage can next to the State Park's visitor's center. Feet are not supposed to feel like this—like they've been hacked at by an axe, chewed up by a beaver, and spit back into my shoes.

I'm pretty sure I've never walked nine and a half miles in a single day, ever in my life. None of the training hikes we did to prepare for this adventure were anywhere near this long. We never even went half this far with full packs on our backs. Mom did a few full-blown training hikes with her pack and poles on, but I mostly just got used to the feel of my hiking pack by wearing it around the house. There was no way I was going to be *that* person, a total nut walking around our busy Minneapolis neighborhood with a pair of unnecessary trekking poles and a giant backpack strapped over my shoulders. There's an older couple who stroll along the creek near my house who sometimes use hiking poles on their walks together, but that's because they're *old*. I just couldn't do it. It was way too embarrassing. But now, after nine-plus miles of extreme trekking, I wish I had.

I sprawl out on a wooden bench inside the park's bustling visitor's center, feet up, not even worried about all the people who are walking by and staring. I'm pretty sure I smell a lot like the inside of my brother's hockey bag—the entire back and pits of my T-shirt are soaked through with sweat. And I'm guessing I look a little terrifying. You're probably not supposed to lie on the benches in the visitor's center lobby, but I really don't care. All I want to do is curl up and moan, and everyone else is just going to need to be okay with that.

Tonight, Mom has reserved us a campsite in the Gooseberry Falls State Park campground, rather than having us sleep out in the middle of nowhere on the Superior Hiking Trail. All along the trail—which runs more than three hundred total miles from start to end, along the north shore of Lake Superior— there are dozens of backwoods campsites that you can sleep at for free. But for our first night out here, Mom and I both thought it would be best if we stayed somewhere with easy water access (yummy drinking fountains!), indoor bathrooms, and a place to shower.

I pull out the slim journal Mom bought for me to bring along on our hike, and glare at it. "You can reflect on your experiences on the trail," she'd suggested, handing it to me as we were finishing up our packing. "Take notes on what we see and how you feel each day." Mom is big on writing stuff down; she teaches fifth grade, and her entire class is forced to journal for ten minutes each morning. Also, she's been seeing a therapist since Dad took off, and the woman she sees has her on some sort of write-out-your-feelings routine.

It's not until I notice that the streak of sunlight has disappeared from the bench beside me that I wonder how long Mom has been gone. She set out to find a park bathroom right after we got inside the visitor's center, leaving me alone with our entire wilderness world stuffed into the two packs perched on the bench beside me. But how long ago was that? I can't help but imagine that the woods might have a side door that she could magically sneak out of to hail a cab home, leaving me stranded out here all by myself. Just like Dad did that day he bailed, but *worse* since Mom's all I have left anymore.

Alone, with no idea how to set up our tent on my own.

Alone, with no clue about what comes next.

Alone, scared, sore, and tired.

Luckily, I'm *pretty* sure there aren't any cabs just hanging around in the middle of nowhere, so hopefully she'll be back soon. We can't quit on day one. We can't quit, *period*. I refuse to give Dad the satisfaction. With a sigh, I open to the journal's first page and stare at the blank lines. I need to write something, anything, to keep my brain from going down the wrong path.

*Day 1: Castle Danger to Gooseberry Falls State Park*, I write, since those are simple facts about where we started and where we finished the day.

*Miles: 10.* We haven't actually gone ten whole miles *yet*

today, but there's going to be another little walk from the visitor's center to the campground. So I'm rounding up. It will be ten miles by the time we set up our tent tonight, and I'm planning to count every single step I take.

*Smell Factor: Jake's hockey bag-level bad.*

"Guess what I found." I hear Mom's voice before I notice that she's returned.

I look up and blurt out, "Did you fall asleep on the toilet or something? Where have you been?" But then I notice what she's holding in her hand, and I immediately forgive her. "Is that . . . ice cream?"

Mom grins. "Hungry?"

"You're a mirage," I say, tossing the journal and my worries about being stranded alone out here to the side. "Is this some kind of trick? Like when people think they see water in the desert, and they run toward it, but when they get there, they get hit with a mouthful of sand?"

Mom pulls the wrapper off a Butterfinger ice cream bar on a stick and wedges it between my fingers. "It's real," she promises, laughing.

I take a bite and the cold, sweet rush feels almost as good as jumping off a dock into a lake on a hot day. There's no better feeling in the world than jumping into water when you're hot, except maybe the feeling of this ice cream bar, right this second. "Mmmm," I sigh, sitting up. "True love. I'm pretty sure I could marry this ice cream. Josephine Butterfinger has a nice ring to it. Regal, even."

The words are out of my mouth before I even realize what I'm saying. We don't talk about marriage. We don't say the words *true love*. Because those things are gone from our house now that the divorce is final. Dad ripped true love into pieces, then stitched the shredded bits back together to create a whole new family.

Mom schlumps down on the bench beside me and quietly bites chunks off her ice cream bar. "I'm sorry," I say, scooting over to lean my head against her shoulder. I don't even know what else to say. We mostly just avoid the subject of Dad, but whenever he *does* come up, I try to make a joke out of it. "I promise if I ever do marry someone with the last name Butterfinger, I'll keep Conlan for myself, okay?"

She snorts quietly.

"If we have kids, they might decide they want to hyphenate their last name, but at least Butterfinger-Conlan works pretty well, don't you think?"

Mom leans her head on mine and doesn't say anything. There's been a lot of saying nothing lately. We *talk* plenty, but don't *say* a whole lot. It's much easier that way. If you don't dwell, it hurts a whole lot less.

When we've finished our ice cream, I grunt and push myself to standing. "How's the bathroom in this place?" I ask Mom. "Was it worth the whole extra quarter-mile walk off the trail to stop by the visitor's center for an indoor toilet that flushes?"

"Totally worth it. And we got ice cream out of the deal,"

Mom says, plugging her phone into an outlet to give it a little juice. "Enjoy the privacy and a toilet seat while you've got them. After tomorrow morning, it's gonna be nothing but open-air latrines for days."

As I hobble to the bathroom, I realize *every* muscle in my body feels like it's been chewed up and spit out by a beaver— it's not just my feet. I'm not sure how I'm supposed to get up tomorrow and do this again.

But I guess that's how it's been for weeks and months. So many other peoples' lives have just kept rolling along the past couple years while ours came skidding to a sudden stop. Yet somehow, every day, Mom and I both manage to get up and keep moving. At least, we have up until now.

But what if this is our breaking point?

What if Mom *does* quit on me . . . on us?

I dig into the knots in my neck with my thumbs. If I feel this bad *now*, how much worse will it be tomorrow and the day after that?

If I just keep moving, maybe it won't hurt so much.

*Just keep walking*, and maybe we can ignore the pain.

Day 1: Castle Danger to Gooseberry Falls State Park
Miles: 10.0
Smell Factor: Jake's hockey bag-level bad

---

# CHAPTER THREE
# MORNING TICKS

"Hold still." Mom's voice is a whisper.

I open my eyes to find her hunched over me with a pair of tweezers, inching toward me in the green-blue light of our tent. I instinctively roll away and cover my face with the long-sleeve shirt I balled up to use as a pillow in the night.

Mom twists her fingers through my bangs and pins me down. "I said, hold *still*."

"I'm sleeping," I grumble. "Go away. Why are you so close to me? It's creepy and I'm pretty sure it's, like, five in the morning."

"It's seven thirty," Mom tells me, her morning breath way too close to my face. "You've got a tick."

"I'm awake!" I screech, immediately sitting upright. I bonk my head on the tiny little solar-powered lantern we hung from the top of our tent last night to keep the dark away. My head *was* the only thing that didn't hurt at the end of our first day of hiking, but now that's gonna hurt, too. "Where is it?"

"Your neck," Mom says, pinching her tweezers at me again. "Right below your ear. It's not in very deep yet, so it should come out pretty easily." She leans forward, and I can feel the cool metal of the tweezers press against my neck.

Slowly, Mom pulls the little bloodsucking creep out of my skin, unzips the screen door, and tosses it out of the tent. I know Mom hates ticks, possibly almost as much as she hates my dad, and that it's probably taking every ounce of will-power for her to do this for me. "Thanks," I say, rubbing my neck gently. "Now can I go back to sleep?"

"No," Mom says. She pops open the air valve on her inflatable sleep mat, and a whoosh of stale air hits me smack in the face. "We should get going, since it's supposed to be hot again today. I have service here, so I checked my weather app. This afternoon is going to be a scorcher." She folds her mat in half and rolls it, then stuffs it in its sack. While I continue to lie there like a dead person, Mom shoves her sleeping bag and spare clothes into a compression sack, and jams everything into her pack. "I'm going to make some coffee, then let's pee, eat, fill up our water bottles, and go."

I manage to give her a double thumbs-up, but don't move more than that.

I'm not sure I can.

# CHAPTER FOUR
# FROZEN ORANGE JUICE

By midafternoon, it's probably close to ninety degrees. We're shooting for a campsite along the Split Rock River tonight, and I'm really hoping it's the kind of river you can swim in. I've never smelled this awful in my entire life. For a moment, I think I might actually be making myself a little sick from my own scent, but then Mom reminds me that it's probably the heat and thirst kicking in.

I can't stop thinking about the ice cream bar from yesterday afternoon.

Can't stop thinking about how much my feet and ankle hurt.

Can't stop thinking about a blue slushy from the gas station near my house.

Can't stop thinking about how much I *don't* want to eat hot, rehydrated lasagna for dinner again tonight, same as last night.

Can't stop thinking about how different this trip would have been with Dad.

A wave of guilt immediately washes over me with that last thought. I am obviously grateful that Mom was willing to join me out here. Especially because this really isn't her kind of adventure.

But this hike was supposed to be something special. It was supposed to be the thing me and Dad did together, until he decided to go to Chicago with Catherine and Ellie and Sam instead. "It's a big celebration trip for Ellie's graduation," Dad had explained when he broke the news to me this spring. "She's leaving for college in the fall, and Catherine wants me to be a part of Ellie's final trip with the family. I just can't take another two weeks off this summer, Jo. We can go on the hike together next year."

"You know how long I've been waiting for this trip with you," I'd whined, hating the sound of my own desperate voice. "Please."

I was almost five when Dad and Jake set off on their big hike together, and I've been waiting for my turn ever since. "The summer before seventh grade," Dad told me, over and over again. "Same as Jake. I promise." But then Catherine and Ellie and Sam entered the picture, and all of Dad's promises melted away.

"Can we stop for a break?" I call out to Mom once I realize how badly I need to get out of my own head. We've already stopped about five times today for "pack off" big breaks, and another dozen or so times for shorter "foot breaks."

We have another nine-and-a-half-mile day planned today,

and the trail is definitely not any easier than yesterday. In fact, today is much, much worse. Somehow, my body magically felt okay when I was lying down this morning, but as soon as I put weight on my feet, it was like someone had quietly but forcefully shoved a small knife up into the bottom of each of my heels. The ankle I twisted yesterday is sore, but even *that* is overshadowed by my stabbing feet and the shooting pain radiating in every direction from my pack's shoulder straps.

I scoped out the map during a break and foolishly assumed that when we reached the chunk of trail that runs along the edge of the Split Rock River, the rest of our day's walk would be pretty flat. But whoever built the Superior Hiking Trail was thoughtful enough to throw all kinds of unnecessary climbs and descents into what could have been a smooth, relaxing walk along the edge of a pretty, burbling river.

Mom shrugs her pack off her shoulders and dumps it on the ground. Then she leans against a tree and moans. "Do you know what I've been thinking about for the past hour?" she asks, reaching into her pack for the last swig of lukewarm water. We filled all our water bottles this morning at the campground's drinking fountain—three liters for each of us—but they're empty already. The only plus to empty water bottles is that it's weight we no longer need to carry. As soon as we get to camp, we'll need to scoop water out of the river and filter it. No more drinking fountains for a while. We only get to drink when we fetch the water ourselves. "I'd give anything for that orange juice they hand out for breakfast at school. You know how sometimes it's still a little frozen, and if you get lucky, it still has icy orange juice shards in it?"

As the kid of a teacher, I always got to go to school early with my mom during elementary school. I memorized the breakfast calendar each week and could always tell my mom which days they were serving her favorites—banana muffins and orange juice. I never thought I'd miss either one of them. But now that Mom brought up the orange juice, I can't stop thinking about the muffins. "Can I tempt you with a chunk of meat stick instead?" I offer. "Or a dried fruit bar?"

Mom sags. "It's really hot."

"Thank you, Captain Obvious," I say in a slightly snippier tone than is probably necessary. "I wonder how much farther to tonight's campsite?"

She consults her app while I pull out the old-fashioned paper map and try to figure out where we are. Dad would have totally rejected the idea of a GPS mapping app, insisting that we leave our phones at home, but Mom refused to consider going on this trip without one. I'll admit, the little blue dot that shows us exactly where we are on the phone's map is a pretty neat feature. "Looks like we're about a mile away from camp. We've gone just short of eight and a half so far today." She gestures to the river, bubbling downstream to our right. "And the water in the river looks deep enough that we might be able to rinse off tonight."

"You're not planning to swim naked, right?" I ask, just to make sure. Neither of us packed a swimsuit, and I suddenly realize what this might possibly mean.

Mom rolls her eyes. "You are an odd duck."

I start to lift my pack off the ground, but the weight of it nearly drags me over. "I volunteer you to carry my pack the rest of the day," I announce, schlumping against a tree.

"Josephine Conlan, I volunteer *you* as tribute," Mom says in a weird accent. "Hunger Games: Minnesota edition. May the odds be ever in your favor."

"You know what?" I say, considering this. "I actually think I would prefer to be in the Hunger Games than to put this pack back on my body again today." As soon as I say it, I realize I mean it. After just two days out here, I'm having trouble remembering exactly why I pushed so hard for this trip to happen. Hiking, as it turns out, is hard, and I really hope it ends up being worth it. Worth the stabbing feet and mosquitoes and ticks; worth wearing clothes that smell like week-old roadkill; worth the hot, thirsty, exhausting days of all this alone time on the trail just to prove we can do this. To prove that we'll *survive*.

We haven't even gone twenty total miles yet, and Mom and I both already look like ice cream in a carton that's been sitting out on the kitchen counter way too long. I can't figure out how we're supposed to make it nearly one hundred more. Would this all be easier if Dad were here? I know I shouldn't wonder that, even inside the secret space of my own head. Even if maybe, possibly, I already know the answer and I don't like it.

"Come on," Mom says, lifting my pack off the ground and gently lowering it onto my shoulders. "Let's keep moving."

# CHAPTER FIVE
# ONLY PEE WHEN YOU'RE DOWNSTREAM

We finally make it to our campsite a little after three. There are four official Superior Hiking Trail sites to choose from along the Split Rock River, and even though we're barely still standing, Mom and I decide to keep walking to one of the farthest ones, since doing so means we'll have fewer miles to walk tomorrow.

No one else is at the campsite when we get there, even though there's enough room for four or five tents, and it begins to dawn on me that we've barely seen anyone since we left the heart of the State Park this morning—just a few day hikers and a small crowd of people taking pictures in front of the waterfall right off the highway. They'd all stared at us, walking past with our giant packs. I have to admit, it was fun to see people sweating and moaning as they climbed a short trail *without* packs on their backs, and then witness their reaction as we come hiking by *with* all our gear. It makes a girl feel pretty tough, to be honest. But the truth is that I'm not tough at all.

I wasn't sure what to expect out here, but I guess I hadn't planned to be so . . . *alone* all day. I'd assumed we'd be passing other hikers all the time, waving and chatting. Part of me imagined we'd stop to have lunch with fellow hikers we bumped into on top of a mountain. Or that a big group of us would sit around a campfire at night—roasting some marshmallows and talking about the best brands of dried fruit or something equally outdoorsy.

But since it's been a super-dry summer in the Midwest, there's a fire ban—so no campfires, and no new friends yet either. Just me and Mom, our dehydrated lasagna, and too much time to think. It's the same level of loneliness we've been living through at home, but out here, there's even more time to notice what's missing. The only good thing about the pain shooting through my feet, ankle, and shoulders is that it's a distraction from some of my worries while we walk.

We get to camp and spend some time wandering around the site to scope it out, eventually picking a flat, dirt-crusted tent pad tucked within a grove of pine trees. While Mom digs out the tent, I head off to find the latrine so I can pee for the first time since this morning. As I drag myself down the latrine trail, I carefully unroll three measly squares of toilet paper from the roll we keep dry inside a little ziplock baggie, since Mom has warned me—repeatedly—that we need to conserve it. I've never thought of toilet paper as a luxury item until now, but that's what happens when you only have one roll of TP to last for five whole days.

And the worst part is, you really don't want to be thinking about *anything* when you're doing your business—speed is key. Campsite toilets are not comfy; they're made of weather proof hard brown plastic, they're right out in the open (no door to close for privacy), and most are swarming with flies since they don't have a toilet seat or cover. I've already discovered that when a latrine *does* have a toilet cover, it's almost worse—since the smell of everything inside the hole gets trapped under the lid and when you open it, the stink wafts out and hits you square in the face.

I pee quick, squirt some hand sanitizer on my hands, stuff the roll of paper back in our plastic baggie, and head toward the main campsite area. Mom already has our tent set up, and she's tossing our sleeping mats and bags inside. I help her hook the rain fly on the tent and stake it down so it won't blow away. We take our water purifier, camp stove, books, and chairs down to the river. The mosquitoes always seem to find us quickly in the woods, but when we take breaks out on the rocks in the middle of a river or on top of a ridge, the wind usually helps to keep them at bay.

I toss my stuff onto a large, dry, flat rock in the middle of the river, and immediately make my way over to a shallow pool created by a wall of rocks. Usually, the Split Rock River would be too wild to swim in. It's stuffed full of huge boulders, and the water cascades over them in varying sizes of rushing waterfalls all along its path. But the one good thing about getting less rain this summer is that all the major rivers along the trail are lower than usual, which is nice for stuff like swimming.

When I was little, Dad used to drive me and Jake up the North Shore for day hikes or weekend car camping trips, and I can remember stopping at the base of the Split Rock River to throw stones. One time, maybe when I was about four, Jake's hat blew off his head and I watched in horror as the river tossed and tumbled it downstream, impossibly fast. It was gone from sight in no time—buried forever under the rushing, pounding water. Dad let Jake pick out a new hat at a gas station later that afternoon, and he let me choose something, too. I picked out a visor that had a see-through red brim, because when I looked up at the sky through that plastic brim, the whole world looked rosy and cheerful. I wonder what ever happened to that visor.

Just down the trail from our campsite, the gentle river weaves and bends through giant rocks, creating waterfalls and pools that are just big enough to sit in and cool off. I decide to test the current by tossing a stick in to see what will happen to it. The stick bobs along, gently floating from pool to pool, passing from tiny waterfall to waterfall, staying within my view for a comfortably long time. Eventually, it slows to a stop inside a larger pool downstream, floating there in lazy circles. The result of this little experiment makes me feel like it's definitely safe to swim. I'm starving, but I don't think I can eat when I smell this bad—so I carefully wade into one of the less mossy-looking pools and ease my body in, clothes and all.

"That looks amazing," Mom says, but doesn't move to join me.

"Come in. It's perfect," I tell her.

Mom shakes her head. "I'm going to filter some more water first."

"Do you want me to fill our bottles? You should swim. It feels *so* good." I hope she says no, but I feel like I need to offer to help, since this is technically *my* trip and I really need to pull my weight on the day's chores, or else she'll quit on me.

"I don't want to get leeches," Mom says, peering into one of the river's deeper pools. "It looks leechy in there."

I glare at her. "*Are* there leeches? Do you actually see any?"

"Probably?" she says. "This looks like the kind of water where leeches would lurk."

I decide to ignore this, and hope leeches are scared off by the salt that is probably still clinging to my body from a day of sweating like a professional soccer player. If she doesn't want to smell better, that's her loss. Though we are sharing one tent and I can pretty much guarantee her body and feet don't smell any better than mine do right now—so it's kind of my loss, too.

I dip my head back into the waterfall behind me, letting the river water rush over me. My clothes are soaked, and for the first time all day, I can't feel my feet and ankle throbbing. But I still can't help thinking about how quickly Dad would have jumped in the water without hesitation. At least in the before times.

When Mom finishes scooping and squeezing water through our filter, she scoots across the rocks toward me and dangles her legs in the pool. She passes me a bottle of water and orders me to drink up. Her eyes drift closed, then she opens them, squints at me, and says, "Any leeches yet?"

I stand up and spin, but since I'm still wearing clothes, we can't see many parts of my skin at all. "Is it okay if I drape my clothes on a rock to dry, and pretend my underwear and sports bra are a swimsuit?" I ask.

"Have you seen the swimsuits some people wear?" Mom asks. "I'm pretty sure you can call *anything* a swimsuit these days."

I tug my sodden hiking pants and T-shirt off, squeeze out as much water as I can, then lay them flat on a sun-covered rock to dry. I sniff my shirt before setting it down, relieved that the river seems to have washed off all the stink. As soon as I'm down to sports bra and underwear—my camping swimsuit—I return to the little pool and settle in under the same waterfall again. The water feels smooth like velvet as it rushes over my bare skin. My entire body was hurting, but the gentle caress of fresh water against my aching muscles is helping me forget how bad today's hike was.

The next time I open my eyes, Mom is slithering in beside

me, wearing her own version of a camp swimsuit. "Still no leeches?" she asks warily.

I start to shake my head no, but then I make a face and scoot away from her. "Um . . . just that huge one, right there," I say, pointing at a spot under her armpit.

Mom screams, batting at her stomach and arms.

"Oh," I moan. "I think it might be a whole family of leeches. They're spreading. Don't move, or you'll anger them."

She's waving her arms so wildly, she loses her balance and her foot slips on a mossy rock. She windmills, flails, and then lands in the deepest part of this section of water on her butt. I really hope she's not hurt, since I can't stop myself from laughing.

"There is no leech, is there?" Mom growls at me, pushing her wet hair out of her eyes.

I smile back. "Not yet."

"You are cruel," she snaps as she settles in beside me. A few minutes later, she asks, "Is it okay if I pee in the water? I'll wade downstream, so it doesn't flow toward you."

"Um . . ." I smile sheepishly. "I maybe already peed a little, right in that spot where you're sitting now. But don't worry! It was a while ago, so it's probably floated about half a mile downstream by now."

Mom closes her eyes and takes a deep breath, laughing in spite of herself. "This is going to be a very long two weeks."

I agree. Then I start to laugh, too, and know that I definitely wouldn't have been able to laugh this hard with Dad.

<u>Day 2</u>: Gooseberry Falls State Park to Split Rock River

<u>Miles</u>: 9.5

<u>Toilet Paper Count</u>: 19 squares total—and it's the thin, scratchy kind that they have at school! (Mom says we need to "use it sparingly" since we only have one roll to share, for five days. I'm keeping count of how much I use, so there's proof it's not my fault if we run out. There are 426 squares on one roll—I Googled it—which means I get 213 and Mom gets 213. If we run out, this journal will show which of us is responsible for using more than her fair share.)

<u>Smell Factor</u>: Here's the thing I'm realizing about deodorant: It doesn't <u>stop</u> the smell or <u>hide</u> the smell. It just sort of mingles with your BO and pretends to mask it—but not well.

<u>Major Pains</u>: My beaver-chewed feet and the stabby ankle. Also, my pack is rubbing a little hole in each of my hip bones where the waist strap wraps around. I covered the spots with Band-Aids, but I think my hips might start bleeding if it rubs any more.

---

# CHAPTER SIX
# *CLINK!*

I drop one shaking knee to the rocky ground and use both hands to push myself up another level of this natural stone staircase. Slowly, I haul my other leg up behind me and try to return to standing. But going from hands and knees to upright is a whole lot harder when you're weighed down by an extra thirty pounds of pack on your back. Mom is already at the top of the climb, waiting, and I quietly growl at her for being *up* when I'm still way too far *down*.

I roll and slide my body and pack up and over a few more boulders, using my hiking poles as an extra set of feet to help get me the rest of the way to the top.

When we were planning this hike, I fought hard to get a walking stick instead of dorky trekking poles. "Like Gandalf would use," I'd argued. "A nice, crooked stick with some *character* will make me feel more legit out there in the woods."

But the lady at the outdoor store who helped outfit us for the trip had told me poles were a must. "You're not that tall," she'd said, which stung. I'm over five feet now, which is taller than a few adults I know. I'm shorter than average for my grade, sure, but being height-challenged is a sensitive topic for someone with two parents and a brother who all tower around six feet. "A good set of poles is going to help you get up and down some of the steep climbs, and will keep you steady on the rockiest parts of the trail."

Over the past few days, I've learned that by tucking the tips of my poles into the small spaces between rocks where my *actual* feet and hands can't fit, I can lean on them and keep my balance a little better on tough climbs and descents. But even with the two extra limbs, I'm so tired and weak after so many miles, I wouldn't be surprised if I suddenly rolled off a rock ledge and went splat on the forest floor below.

I glare up at my mom's long legs. "Do you have any idea how much harder these climbs are for someone my size?"

Mom looks down at me from the top and chews her lip. "I'd offer to help, but . . ." I am still looking up at her when she unscrews the cap of her water bottle and takes a swig, as if to torture me even further. I look at her just long enough that I don't place my next foothold quite right, and my knee slams into the solid rock that is—luckily—only a few inches below where I'm hovering. Still, I can feel the burn in my knee and stinging in my eyes as tears threaten to spill.

*Don't cry.*
*Don't cry.*
*Don't cry.*

"If I die on my way up this awful hill, you better finish this stupid hike for both of us," I snap.

"If you die on this hill," Mom says, "I'm ditching my pack right here and *running* for the nearest road. If I can get cell service, I'll call a helicopter to pull me out. Whatever gets me out of the woods the fastest."

I hate when she says stuff like this. As if I don't already know Mom's only out here for me.

I hate that I dragged her out here. I hate that Dad let us *both* down by bailing. I hate that she hates everything about this adventure.

And today, I hate this trail just as much as she does. I'm not exactly in what you'd call "fighting shape" and that's become pretty obvious these past few days. I'm in *"reading* shape," which doesn't help launch you up a hill.

When I get to the top, I push past my mom and keep walking, leaving her to stash her water bottle in her pack by herself and hustle along after me.

Back when this trip was still just in the prep stages, had I envisioned a nice, relaxing hike through the woods, on a wood-chip-lined trail with a few get-your-heart-pounding gentle hills? Maybe. Had I expected major bouldering, parts of the trail where I would literally have to get on my hands and knees and hoist myself up onto ginormous rock after ginormous rock? Not exactly. So maybe the outdoor store lady was right. Because yeah, the poles do come in handy— sometimes. Not when I'm literally on hands and knees trying to *roll* up a mountain, but most of the rest of the time that spare set of limbs does help.

The problem with hiking poles, though, is the sound they make. Straight out of the package, my poles came with a cute set of little rubber nubs on the bottom that kept them from getting stuck in the dirt or sliding on rocks. But the nubs fell off sometime on our first day out here, and the bottom of each pole is now just a pointy, metal spike. All day long: *clink, clink, clink, clink.*

With each step I've taken today on the rocky path leading up and away from Split Rock River, my poles land with a solid *clink* on rock. It's pretty much the only sound I hear, other than the song Mom is alternately whistling and humming as we hike. Today's tune is "Under the Sea" from *The Little Mermaid*, on repeat. *The Little Mermaid* is her favorite Disney movie, so she often sings songs from the movie when we're driving in the car. It was annoying then; now, her nonstop Disney songs are making me downright angry. But the thing about walking all day long is, if you get a song stuck in your head, there's not much you can do to get it back *out* again.

If I'm not careful, I'll *also* be singing Disney songs on repeat right along with her. I focus instead on the sound of my poles.

*Clink!*

*Clink!*

*Clink!*

The sound reminds me of people clinking champagne glasses at a wedding, and suddenly, I'm transported back to

35

the night of my parents' twentieth wedding anniversary party. They'd rented the back room at their favorite restaurant and invited fifty people to celebrate with them. Jake came home from college—he'd only been gone from home a few months at that point, but I missed him like crazy already—and there were appetizers and fizzy drinks and a giant cake decorated to look like an elaborate sandcastle, because my parents got married on the beach.

Dad had hired a small jazz band to play some of Mom's favorite songs, as a special surprise. They danced, and he dipped her, and I thought how sweet—and how *embarrassing*—it was that my parents were making this big show of demonstrating their very rusty foxtrot skills and cringey romance. After he finished dancing with Mom, Dad had swept over to me, bowed like some sort of king, and asked, "May I have this dance?" Meanwhile Mom swirled around the dance floor with Jake, and everyone cheered and joined us as Louis Armstrong sang about what a wonderful world it was, and I was so, so happy.

Thinking back, that might have been the last night we were all together, all happy. Now, not even two years later, it seems crazy that we were ever a family like that. That happy, or that together. I wonder if my dad was already dating Catherine by then, and if he felt bad for clinking glasses and yelling "cheers!" and kissing my mom when he should have known he was a total jerk who was planning to abandon his family.

*Clink*, goes my pole.

*Clink.*

*Clink.*

I wonder if he knew that what he was doing would break my mom into a million little pieces. I wonder if he knew Jake would stop coming home after that, since home wasn't even home anymore. I wonder if he already knew then that he was going to bail on our hike, our life, our family. I wonder if he knew he had the power to destroy our world.

I hate him.

*Clink.*

*Clink.*

*Clink.*

He's already taken everything from us, so I'm not letting him ruin this hike, too. But now that it's in my head, I can't stop thinking about that night. All those smiling faces, mine included, gazing at my parents as they clinked their glasses and celebrated twenty happy years together. *Cheers!*

I hate him.

No, I *want* to hate him, but in this moment all I can see is the smile on his face while he was dancing with me. Then I think about the way he ran his hand through my mom's hair, rubbed the soft spot under her ear, as she cut into that sand-castle cake. And I remember the tears that ran down his cheeks as we drove away the first time we left Jake at his dorm for college.

*Clink.*

*Clink.*

*Clink*.

With each step, I slam the tips of my hiking poles against the rocky ground, trying to bust through and smash the memories. Dad took twenty years and erased them, like the surf that rolls in and washes away the sandcastles on a beach each night. No trace of the foundation left, no thought for all the work that was put into building it, no tears for everything that's suddenly just *gone*.

I bet Dad has no regrets about all the things he stole from us.

I hate him, and I hate that he broke everything and left me and Mom to clean up the pieces.

I hate that I already want to quit this stupid hike, since it makes me think of Dad and how much easier this whole thing would be if he were here.

I hate myself for thinking that.

"I have to stop for a snack. Okay?" Mom asks, but she's already pulling her pack off her back.

We've been walking along a ridge ever since the killer climb, and now thousands of trees sway majestically all around us. It's another steamy day, but up here, at least there's enough wind to keep me from feeling like I'm hiking in a sauna. Mom groans and says, "Now *I* might be dying."

I shove all that Dad-hate deep down and smile at my mom, trying to be strong for both of us. "Snickers bar, or dried apples?" I make a retching sound. Putting the chewy, dried apples in our pack was maybe a good *effort* on Mom's part, but they will always be a last-choice snack food.

"Snickers," Mom says. "Obviously."

We plunk down on the ground, backs leaning against our packs. "You really think we're going to make it more than one hundred miles?" I ask, taking a massive bite of my candy bar.

"No," Mom says. "Yes? Maybe."

"Which one?"

"I don't know," she says honestly. "This is hard, Jojo. And have you seen all the bear poop on the trail today?"

"Scat."

"What?"

"It's called bear *scat*," I say. The big mounds of berry-filled poop that litter the trail and look—to me—like little melting Jabba the Hutts are called scat. I learned this from Dad, but I'm not going to tell Mom that. "Cute word for poop, huh?"

"No," Mom says, crumpling up her empty candy wrapper—with the melty-chocolate bits tucked safely on the inside—before shoving it deep inside her pocket. We'll have to seal it up inside our food bag tonight, since bears and critters can apparently sniff out even the tiniest hint of leftover food smell. "It's not cute at all. And I'll just tell you now, if we see a bear, that's *definitely* it for me. I'm out of here."

I clench my teeth, resisting the urge to roll my eyes.

But bears are a real concern. There are plenty out here in these woods, and that's why we have to put our food away safely every night. To make it easier, Mom bought some sort of overpriced bear-proof bag that prevents bears from getting your food if you tie it tightly to a tree, as well as a couple very expensive zip-up baggie things that are supposed to keep animals from ever smelling any of your human food in the first place.

When I foolishly told Dad about the bear bag and the fancy plastic bags, he scoffed and said they were a waste of money. He said true hikers know how to tie a bear bag high in a tree, and the supplies Mom bought are silly. That's when I vowed never to tell him anything else about our hike; he gave up his right to comment when he bailed on our trip.

"They're not grizzlies," I remind Mom. "We just have black bears out here. It's highly unlikely they'll rip us and our tent to shreds."

She whimpers. "How comforting." We lay there in the middle of the trail in silence, looking up at the clouds overhead, letting the wind and sunshine dry some of the sweat off the front of our T-shirts. Eventually, Mom turns her head to look at me and says quietly, "I'm kind of surprised we've made it this far, to tell you the truth."

I turn my head to look back at her. "Me, too."

"I figured three days, tops, and we'd bail," she confesses. "But we haven't, and that's pretty cool."

I had kind of assumed the same thing. Though I've been on plenty of weekend camping trips with Dad over the years, neither Mom nor I really knows what we're doing on this kind of adventure. Dealing with a bear bag,

**40**

filtering water, hiking day after day, setting up a tent on our own, using a camp stove—that's all new to both of us. We each read a half dozen hiking guidebooks, we took some practice walks, did a couple overnights in a state park campground, and Mom went to a few evening presentations at REI. But all those things together don't add up to solid trail experience.

Here's a truth about Mom: She's not exactly what you'd call a *rugged* outdoors person. My mom is more of a sit-on-the-end-of-a-dock-and-read kind of nature-lover. She likes to *see* wilderness and be outdoors, but not necessarily soak herself in it.

Unlike Dad, who grew up canoeing and fishing and camping and is the kind of guy who loves to be outside in the garden, even if it means getting bit by sandflies all afternoon. He can be bleeding from all those bites, and not even be bothered by it. That's why Dad took Jake on this same big adventure when my brother was my age, and that's why he was the one who was going to take me. Dad knows stuff about the woods, and survival, and he's not scared of things like leeches and ticks and bears and bleeding from bug bites.

But here's a truth about Mom *now*: She's the one who's out here, hiking and camping and hurting with me. Dodging bear scat and getting it done.

Unlike Dad, who hasn't been camping in over a year. His garden is empty this summer. No jalapeño peppers, or gourds, or zinnias, or tomatoes, or basil are growing—it's just weedy soil. Dad's too busy growing a new family to grow veggies, and he traded his sleeping bag for a fancy hotel room in Chicago.

So even if she's not loving this adventure, the most important truth about Mom is: She's the one willing to sleep under the stars, surrounded by bugs and predators and a trail that's trying to kill us, just so I don't have to give up on the hike I've been waiting years to take. She might not love it, but at least she's *here* for me.

We're doing it.

I just know that if we can survive this, together, we can survive anything.

Mom pulls our water bottles out of the side pockets of our packs and passes one to me. She holds hers in the air between us, knocking it against mine. "Cheers," she says with a smile that is exactly what I need to see to get me through the next few miles. "To us, and the fact that we're still walking. We haven't quit yet."

# CHAPTER SEVEN
# CAR CAMPING VS. TRAIL CAMPING

The summer after I turned seven, just before Jake started high school, our family rented an RV and took a road trip to Michigan. We brought along a grill, and floaties for the beaches we passed, and had our bikes hitched to the back of our big beast of a truck so my brother and I could set out alone to explore the different campgrounds we stayed in. Each night, we'd light a campfire in a metal ring at our site and roast marshmallows for s'mores over the fire. The back of the RV was stuffed with folding chairs, a big bin of snacks, extra towels, Jake's golf clubs (just in case), and a box of books to keep us busy for the week.

Inside the RV, there was a separate bedroom with a door for Mom and Dad, and a cozy, curtained bed nook over the driver's seat for Jake. The "kitchen" table folded down to create a little bed for me right in the center of everything. I loved sleeping in that spot, snuggled in between my brother and my parents, with the sounds of the campground around me. At night, after we'd all tucked in for the night with the windows open to enjoy the cool nighttime air, I could hear distant laughter and sometimes singing or the sound of a strumming guitar from the neighboring campsites. In the morning, I'd lie in bed and listen to the campground waking up around me: slamming RV doors, zipping tent flies, chittering squirrels, and families calling out to one another as they packed, or headed for the showers, or set off on their day's adventures.

As I mentally prepared for this trip, I guess *that* trip sort of blended in with all our tent camping weekends to give me the wrong idea of what to expect. Every time we've camped before now, we've had seemingly endless resources—clean clothes, plenty of fresh water, lots of food options, access to a shower, a toilet that flushes, a Frisbee and a Spikeball set, board games, and a fat stack of books to suit any mood. Out here on the trail, we have none of that. We just have one measly change of clothes, exactly the right amount of food for five days, and a single book that—if I can even stay awake long enough to read at night—I have no choice but to be in the mood for.

We also don't have Dad, or Jake, or the togetherness that came with all those other camping adventures. It's just me and Mom, miles of empty trail, and too much time to think about what's missing and why we're out here. If I'd never traveled in an RV or stayed at a state park campground before, I wouldn't notice all the things we don't have on this camping trip. But I have, so I do. It's sort of like my family: If we'd never been happy, and if we'd never been a perfect mix of Mom plus Dad plus Jake plus me, I wouldn't realize how much worse it is to *not* have those things now.

But I do know what it's like to be that kind of family. I know what it's like to have a fun brother living at home, and a dad who's around on the weeknights, and a mom who goes out with friends and smiles all the time and doesn't need me to hold her up. I know what it's like to spend time hanging out with my friends on the weekend, instead of turning down plans so neither Mom nor I needs to be alone in the house more than is absolutely necessary.

But most importantly, I know what it's like to not be afraid of being alone.

# CHAPTER EIGHT
# SITTING OUT A STORM

It starts drizzling around two. By two thirty, it's flat-out *pouring*. We hastily pull out our backpack rain covers, hooking them on to keep our stuff from getting soaked. We look like neon turtles, with our packs all wrapped up in bright green and orange. Unfortunately, the pack covers do nothing to keep *us* from getting wet, and there's no way I'm wearing rain gear when it's this hot out.

For the first fifteen minutes, the rain feels sort of good—a relief from pure, pounding heat and sunshine. But when my shoes start squelching with each step, I am no longer impressed. My socks start to rub my already aching feet, and the bottoms of my shoes feel sort of squishy and spongy in an unpleasant way.

I can hear the distant rumble of thunder, way off in the distance, and I'm pretty sure we still have about six miles left to hike today if we want to make it to our planned meetup spot by day five. Mom's friend Gina is scheduled to drop off our first resupply box, and if we don't make it, we'll run out of food. We decided to try to jam in an extra-long day today, so we can just hike six tomorrow. According to the map and the guidebook, today's hike is supposed to be flat and pleasant—but the last five or so miles tomorrow is going to be all climbing.

"There's a biggish campsite about a mile up," Mom tells me, after we pass a murky beaver pond and dive back under the cover of woods. We stopped briefly at a trail campsite next to the pond, to pee in the world's grossest latrine, and also to dredge some sludgy-looking water just in case we don't find another drinking water resupply spot today. "If this rain doesn't stop, maybe we should cut early today and just force ourselves to go a little farther tomorrow?"

"Yeah," I agree. The idea of a long day tomorrow doesn't sound great, but neither does another six miles in pounding rain today. To be honest, I just want to curl up on the couch and watch *The Lord of the Rings*. I'd rather not hike any more miles today, or tomorrow, or ever—but that's not an option.

We trudge along for the next forty-five minutes with our heads down, each of us lost in our own brains. I wonder what Mom's thinking about. She hasn't cried yet on our trip, but I have a feeling it's coming. Under the cover of rain, I finally let a few of my own tears fall, comforted by the fact that no one will ever know because my face is already so wet.

One thing that's the same out here as it is at home: I miss my friends, I miss my brother, and even though I really don't want to, I miss my dad. I know it's my own fault that I haven't seen my friends as much lately—I just don't ever want to leave Mom at home alone, since I know how awful it is when she does the same to me. I also know it's not my brother's fault that the timing worked out the way it did, leaving me on my own to figure this stuff out while he went off to college—but it makes me sad just the same.

And Dad? Well, I miss the *old* Dad and the way life used to be. I miss the way it felt when we were all at home together, watching a movie or playing cards or sorting pieces for one of Dad's ugly nature puzzles. I miss never worrying about coming home to an empty house, and I miss the feeling of everything and everyone being in its place. I miss the before, when I wasn't ever afraid of being left alone.

Luckily, I'm never *completely* alone on the trail because Mom is always just a few steps in front of me. But I still feel lonely. We've only been gone from home for three and a half days, but I somehow feel completely disconnected from every part of my real life. I speed up to catch Mom, terrified that we'll somehow lose sight of each other in the rain. The idea of being lost out here, totally alone, is *almost* enough to make me choke out a noisy sob. But I hold it in, knowing I have to stay tough for both of us.

We won't quit.

We can't quit.

As we get close to the Fault Line Creek campsite, the rain slows to a drizzle—but thunder still rumbles in the distance. We pass over a series of mountain bike trails. There are times when our path crisscrosses another path and it's hard to know if we're still walking on the right one. I keep my eye out for the bright blue rectangles—called *blazes*—painted on trees that mark our trail, but sometimes there isn't one when you really need it. Several times, Mom pulls out her phone to check that the blue dot that marks our spot in her app is still on course. She's stopped consulting me on the route today, but I think it's because we're both at our breaking points and want to get our tent set up and put on dry socks before the rain starts up again in earnest. I'm glad she's here to help figure it out, because if it were up to me and me alone right now, I think I might just plop down on my butt on the trail and cry.

Suddenly, I hear voices coming from up ahead. After the past few hours of total loneliness, I've never been so excited to hear the sound of other humans. The sign announcing the Fault Line Creek campsite comes into view, and we turn off the main trail and head toward home-for-the-night.

"Howdy!" I hear as we trudge into camp.

There's a group of three people, two guys and a woman, all of whom are older than my brother but younger than my parents. They're sitting in the middle of the campsite, perched on log benches around an unlit fire pit. There's a big, shorthaired brown-and-white dog lying in between the woman's feet that lifts its head and thumps its tail twice as we walk toward them.

"It's a wet one out here today," one of the guys says, laughing. His long, scruffy dark hair is partially hidden by a baseball cap with a picture of mountains on it, and he has a bright smile that fills most of his face.

"Yeah," I agree, deciding it might be rude if I call *him* Captain Obvious. My bangs are stuck to my forehead, and my pants are so wet and weighed down that the cuffs are dragging on the ground. "Are you staying at this site tonight, too?" I ask hopefully.

Mom *looks* exhausted, and I know she must be, since she doesn't even bother trying to act friendly or introduce herself. In my experience, teachers always seem to be good at greeting new people, even when they're not feeling very social. But not Mom. Not today. She dumps her sodden pack on the ground and pulls the cover off, riffling around inside one of the side compartments for a snack and our camp towel.

"We're thru-hiking south," the woman tells us. She has her light brown hair in two long, messy braids, and is wearing a bright yellow rain jacket that looks to be a few sizes too big on her. I wish Mom or I could braid hair, so I could wear mine like that. Instead, my hair just hangs in wet, mud-brown clumps and tangles around my face, like always. "We were planning to keep going a few more miles today, but decided to wait out the storm here," the stranger says. She points in the direction I think is east. "If those clouds keep heading our way, though, I think we'll probably set up camp and be bunkmates with you for the night. I'm Molly."

"Jo," I tell her, gesturing to myself. "That's my mom, Sarah."

"He's Ben," she tells me, pointing to the guy who hasn't

spoken yet. Ben is very skinny with short, light hair and is wearing the same exact trail shoes as my mom. Then Molly gestures to the guy I've dubbed Captain Obvious and says, "And that's Boots."

"Boots?" I ask, taking a seat on the other log bench. I reach out a hand to let the dog sniff me. "Is your dog friendly?"

"It's the trail name I got when I was hiking on the Appalachian Trail," Boots explains. "My real name's Omar. I'll answer to either. And yeah, Thorin's super friendly. Beat, but friendly."

I stretch my arm farther to rub between Thorin's ears. "Did you name him after the character in *The Hobbit*?"

Omar—*Boots*—nods. "He's my adventure-buddy. We've hiked all over the US together. Did a big chunk of the Appalachian Trail last year, hit up part of the Pacific Crest Trail a few years back when he was still a pup. I take him everywhere. But whenever Molly's out with us, she becomes the favorite. This dog's a total traitor."

Thorin squirms across the ground, bringing his head closer to my hand. Then he lazily stands up, hobbles the rest of the way over to me, and plunks down in a heap at my feet. I grin at Mom, since she loves dogs almost as much as I do, but she's got her head in her hands and is staring down at the ground.

"Thorin knows a *Hobbit* fan when he sees one," I say. I pull out my battered copy of the book to show them what I'm reading—for the thirtieth time—then slip it back into my bag under the rain cover, so it won't get wet.

"Nice." Omar nods approvingly.

"So how long have you two been out here?" Molly asks.

I scoot down to the sloppy ground to be closer to the dog. It's worth it, since I'm already soaked through anyway. His warm body feels like an electric blanket on a cold night, and as I wrap my arms around Thorin's dirty coat, I realize that I'm a little chilly for the first time in three days. It's still drizzling, just a bit, but we're all wet and filthy already, so it really doesn't matter that we're hanging out, chatting, in the rain. "This is our third night," I tell them.

"Feels like a month," Mom grumbles, finally speaking up for the first time since we got to camp. She takes a handful of trail mix—I'm guessing she couldn't find the candy bar stash fast enough—and closes her eyes again. All the positive vibes from earlier in the day seem to have evaporated with the rain, making it clear once again how much she'd rather be anywhere else.

Our three new friends laugh while I try to keep myself from sighing. "How far are you planning to go?" Sarah asks. Ben still hasn't said anything, but I can tell he's listening. He reminds me of the me from school. I don't talk much, but I listen plenty.

I *think* they're all together, but suddenly I realize I have no clue. It's clear from the way they talk that Omar and Molly know each other, but Ben's a mystery. They could be relatives, or a trio of friends, or roommates, or coworkers, or a married couple plus a friend and a dog. They could be running from the law, or recovering from a breakup, or trying to write poetry, or hoping to hide from something or someone, or a collection of strangers who needed a getaway out in nature and are hiking together to avoid having to be out here alone. It actually doesn't matter why they're hiking or who they are; what matters is they're *here* on a night when I really didn't want to be alone.

"About two weeks," I tell them. "We're shooting for just over one hundred miles."

"Nice," Molly says, nodding. She pulls out a pocketknife and starts to whittle the end of a stick. "Where'd you start?"

"Castle Danger trailhead," I answer for both of us, since it's clear Mom doesn't feel like adding much to this conversation. "We're trying to make it to Lutsen." Dad and Jake stopped just *short* of Lutsen Mountains, at a place called Onion River, so that's how I set our goal for the trip. Also, Mom found out you can hike down this spur trail and get to a gondola at the Lutsen ski area. Then you get to *ride* in a little glass-encased bubble down the mountain, and we decided that seems like a pretty neat way to finish our journey.

"Nice," Molly says again.

"We'll be lucky to make it through the week," Mom mutters, then starts to pull our tent out of her pack. "Give me the poles, will you, Jo? I'm going to set up the tent while there's a break in the rain." I dig in my pack and hand her the bag of poles, then attempt to flash an encouraging smile, but she doesn't notice.

"The first few days are the worst," Omar says, ignoring

Mom's bad manners. I suspect everyone gets these moods on the trail, and maybe everyone understands exactly why she's acting the way she is. But it's still weird, annoying really, seeing my usually friendly mom acting like a full-on grump. At least she's not crying. And she hasn't quit. Yet. "But then you get your trail legs and settle into a routine, and you'll start to enjoy yourself."

I sure hope that's true. "You want a hand getting the tent up?" I ask Mom, attempting to bend my legs so I can stand to help. Thorin grunts in protest.

She shakes her head. "To be honest, I could use some alone time," she grumbles. "I'm going to set up the tent, dry off, and lie down for a bit."

Thorin nudges my hand with his nose, and I realize I've stopped petting him to watch Mom. I stroke one of his velvety ears, and he nuzzles in closer. I notice Mom chooses a grassy spot, far away from the unlit campfire ring where we're all sitting, to set up our tent. Then she disappears, leaving me with our new friends.

For a long time after, the only sound is the soft *flick-flick* of Molly's knife on wood as she whittles, Thorin's happy moans, and the soft patter of a gentle rain on the leaves overhead. I want to feel angry at Mom for totally checking out and acting kind of like a jerk. But instead, I find myself feeling grateful for the current company. I rub Thorin's ears and close my eyes, listening. Usually, this would be the kind of quiet that makes me uncomfortable, but out here, with these strangers who don't really feel like strangers at all anymore, it feels . . . okay. And after a day like today, I'll totally take okay.

Day 3: Split Rock River to Fault Line Creek
Miles: 8 miles
Toilet Paper Count: 25 (Confession: I used a few squares to dry off the rim of the latrine so I wouldn't have to sit in a pond to pee.)
Smell Factor: Not roses, that's for sure. And I'm also rocking a kind of "wet dog" odor today.
Major Pains: My whole lower body. I'm also pretty thirsty, but don't want to empty the last of my bottle of good water and dig into the beaver pond sludge.
Day's Soundtrack: "Under the Sea" from The Little Mermaid (Mom's fave)

---

# CHAPTER NINE
# I AM A RAISIN

When I wake up on day four of our hike, Thorin and his humans are already gone from camp. The rain has finally stopped and the sky looks clear, but our stuff is all absolutely soaked.

"Let's just shove it in our stuff sacks wet," Mom says, her voice rough from sleep. "We can stop later and try to dry everything in the sun."

Last night, Mom and I exchanged a total of ten words between arriving at the campsite and turning off our lantern to sleep. "I'm going for last-chance pee," were my words. And hers: "Turn off the lantern."

Maybe having Molly, Omar, Ben, and Thorin in our site with us somehow gave her permission to stop feeling like she needed to fill the silence with mindless chatter. Maybe she was missing Dad, the *old* Dad, just like I was. Maybe the rain was her last straw, and she's just working up the courage to tell me she's done. If that's the case, then I'll just have to avoid talking to her for as long as I can. Whatever the reason for her silence, we somehow navigated dinner, our bed setup, and a whole evening of hiding out inside the tent without forcing any conversation at all. I guess the most important thing is, we survived another day.

Yesterday afternoon, while Mom took time to relax in the tent, I set up the cook stove and made our nightly dehydrated meal. There were two lasagnas and a pesto pasta left to choose from in the food pack. I picked the pesto. While we ate, we sat around the unlit fire with our friends-for-the-night. The three of them chatted amongst themselves, and sometimes with me. I learned that Ben sells insurance and because of his job, he's only out on the trail with the other two for a few days. Molly is Ben's sister, and she's between jobs, which is why she has time to do this thru-hike with Omar. Ben and Omar used to be college roommates, a long time ago, but it's obvious to me that Molly and Omar get along better than Ben does with either Molly or Omar these days.

I'm glad they didn't ask us any questions because I didn't feel like telling them our story.

As soon as we finished eating, Mom shoved all our food and garbage into the bear bag and got that put away for the night while I packed up the stove, put on dry socks and underwear and clothes, and brushed my teeth (I had to skip toothpaste, since that went into the bear bag with all the food). I dumped all my wet stuff in a pile on the ground next to our tent since there wasn't anywhere else to put it.

When I was heading to the latrine before bed, I noticed

that Omar had put up a little tent that he and Thorin share on the trail and discovered that Molly and Ben both sleep in hammocks when they hike. They had a whole setup that didn't look very comfortable or dry to me, but Molly insisted it beat sleeping on the wet ground and made it easier to be able to camp pretty much anywhere. Ben didn't say anything. He just slipped off to pee in the woods and then tucked into his hammock for the night.

Now, with the sun up, I'm feeling pretty well rested but way more sore than any other day so far. We fell asleep early to the sound of rain pattering on the fabric of our tent all night like the white noise rain app my friend Sylvia likes to fall asleep to, but ours was the *actual* sound instead of a recording. And even though Mom and I still haven't said a word to each other, I realize that I don't have that feeling of loneliness that I've woken up with on other days. At least not yet.

The five or so miles between our campsite and Beaver River—the spot where we'd been planning to hike to yesterday—are pretty flat. It only takes a couple hours to get there, but I'm bummed that the rain kept us from making it this far last night, because *now* we have to hike *really* far, and it's obvious neither Mom nor I is in the mood for that. Especially not Mom. I guess the plus of stopping where we did last night is that we met Omar and Molly and Ben and Thorin, and without them, last night would have been way too silent. Plus, it was nice to finally spend a night with someone other than just my mom out here on the trail.

When we reach Beaver River, I'm completely out of yummy drinking water. I'm still lugging a bottle full of pond sludge that we collected yesterday afternoon in the rain, but I've tried to conserve the clean water I had left so I don't have to filter and drink that. Water from beaver ponds is usually brownish and gross, and while it's actually fine to drink it after running it through the filter, it's neither tasty nor yummy looking.

"Should we stop here for a while and dry stuff in the sun?" I suggest, hoping that Mom's mood has improved. The longer I wait for her to cheer up, the more frustrated I become. Shouldn't *I* be the one who gets to act like a pouty teenager?

It's noon, and the sun is warm overhead—though not as hot as it's been previous days, thank goodness—so it feels like the perfect place for a lunch break. "I'm hungry and need some new water." My voice cracks since I haven't used it much this morning. We've walked in silence for most of the day and Mom still seems out of it. We're not even half-way to where we need to get tonight, and I'm already pooped. Luckily, Beaver River looks nothing like yesterday's beaver pond—the water is clear and icy cold.

"Yeah," Mom agrees, and dumps her pack onto a rock alongside the river.

"Are you okay?" I ask softly, hoping this isn't the moment she chooses to tell me she's done.

"Just tired," Mom says. "And sore. And—" She stops short, then adds, "Sorry I'm not great company today."

"You don't have to be great company," I say. "Yesterday was bad."

Mom opens her mouth as if to say something, but then she gives me a thin-lipped smile instead. A few seconds later she says, "Yeah."

While my mom starts dragging the wet tent out of her pack, I slip my shoes and socks off to cool my feet in the river. This morning, my first blister announced itself. When we stopped for a snack and drink earlier, I tried to cover it with a bandage. But just about a mile later, I could feel the bandage sliding around in my sock. Now my whole foot is hot and red and tender, like I've been resting it in burning coals. The blister has popped, and bits of thin skin are peeling away at the edges. How can something so small hurt so bad? I feel the pain shooting all the way up my foot and into my ankle.

I leave my feet in the water until my toes look like raisins, then pop on my Crocs to give my feet a break from socks, being careful not to let the rubber strap touch my heel. Mom rests on a rock while I unpack the rest of our wet gear and drape it across the huge, lichen-covered rocks that jut out from the burbling river. I put my wet clothes in the sunniest spots, hoping stuff will dry so I have something to use as a pillow tonight. By far the *biggest* advantage to making it to Bear Lake tonight is that the campsite is on one end of a big, deep lake. I don't think I can zip myself into the tent again without washing off some of the grime. My body might

**60**

actually be rotting from the outside-in because I'm so smelly and dirty.

"Seven miles left to go today," Mom tells me, consulting her phone map.

I checked the paper map the last time we stopped for a drink, and already know that. But I nod anyway and give her a hopeful smile. There are other places we *could* stop to sleep for the night, before we get to Bear Lake. But stopping early today would leave us with an impossibly long day tomorrow. We're scheduled to meet Regina in a parking lot at three o'clock tomorrow afternoon, to pick up our first resupply box. If there even is a resupply box.

Or is it just Mom's getaway car?

We could have shipped both of our replenishment food boxes to ourselves in some of the towns near the trail, but Gina offered to help us out with this first box, and we weren't going to say no to that level of kindness. We knew it would save us from having to hike extra miles off the trail to get into a town, and we both knew that if we went into a town, we might not be willing to go back out into the woods again.

Because I helped pack it, I happen to know there are Pop-Tarts in the resupply box, and a whole week's worth of Salted Nut Roll candy bars (which might be the only type of candy bar that doesn't melt and turn into baby-poop-looking mush on the trail). The best candy bars are gone from our food bag, and we only have plain instant oatmeal left for breakfast tomorrow. We need this resupply box, and besides, Gina is planning to meet us. So we really can't afford to mess up our schedule any more at this point.

"Are you going to make it that far?" I ask Mom, not wanting her honest answer. Based on how she's been acting this morning and last night, I'm worried her answer is *no*, and I don't want to hear it. I need her to give me a Mom-answer right now, the kind of answer that makes me feel better and reassures me, even if it's not the honest truth.

"I hope so?" Mom says, which is neither an honest answer nor a Mom-answer. I'll take it.

"If the rest of today's hike is like this morning," I say, "we'll be fine."

• • •

News flash: We are not fine.

In fact, I'm pretty sure I might be dying. If twelve-year-olds can have heart attacks, I am a prime candidate for having one right about now.

"We should not have sat and rested at the river so long," Mom huffs as we scramble up another giant rock. "According to my app, we're averaging less than a mile an hour now."

"I didn't need an app to tell me that," I growl back. "But if we hadn't sat at the river so long, we'd still be lugging packs full of soaking wet gear. Our tent is dry, and so is my backup underwear."

Mom laughs, but it only lasts for a second before the unrelenting sun burns the sound away. That's how hot it is.

Our entire afternoon has been filled with never-ending

ups and downs. We spent nearly an hour climbing a huge, rocky mountain and celebrated when we were sure we'd finally reached the tippy-top. The views were stunning, and there were no points higher than us that we could see for miles around. So we figured it was safe to assume we'd spend the next hour or so on flats and downhills. We figured wrong.

Because ever since we got to what we thought was "the top," this stupid trail has been leading us along a ridge that is a nonstop series of clamoring down, then trudging back up, then bumping down again. My knee aches from all the huge boulder steps I've had to climb, and the only good thing is that *that* pain is kind of helping me forget about the blister pain and my ankle and the stabbing feet.

I keep hoping the sun will just go away for a few minutes, but there hasn't been one wisp of cloud. Up here, there aren't even any treetops to create shade, and I'm starting to think I might just want to lie down and let the sun wilt me into a raisin.

*Would* I turn into a raisin?

While I climb, then scoot down, then heave myself back up another pile of rocks, I wonder: What would a seventh-grade, not-very-in-shape, kind-of-introverted, book-loving hiker become if she was wilted by the sun?

A grape becomes a raisin.

An apricot becomes a *dried* apricot.

Lasagna turns into semi-edible dehydrated lasagna-like *crumbles*.

Would I become a shrunken head on a spindly body? I remember reading once that a human body is made up of, like, 60 percent water. So, if I got dehydrated by the sun, would I end up 40 percent of my original size?

I realize a bear would probably eat me long before the sun had time to work its magic. Or a wolf. Or possibly a hawk. Hawks can be fierce. This thought is not comforting.

"Can you check to see how much farther we have to go today?" I ask Mom, stopping to take a swig of water. I've already lost all interest in lying down to be dehydrated by the sun. Now I desperately want to make it to Bear Lake, so I can dunk myself in icy cold water and rehydrate as much as possible.

"I don't think we want to know," Mom says, draining one of her water bottles.

"Yeah," I agree. "You're probably right."

Mom bends at the waist, releasing some of the pack weight from her shoulders and shifting it onto her legs and back. "I'm struggling," she says softly. "I don't know how Tim has done trips like this so many times in his life. It's awful. I'm not sure how much longer I'm going to make it, Jojo."

*Tim.* Mom doesn't say Dad's name very often, so her comment takes me by surprise. "Today?" I ask. "Or in general? Are you saying you don't know how much farther you're going to be willing to hike *overall*?"

"Yeah," she says, wilting to the ground. We're in a part of the trail that's baking in full sun. Generally, we try to only stop to rest in shady or windy spots, to get a break from the heat—but it's clear that Mom isn't going another step until she's rested awhile. "I mean, I might need to be done. I can't do this, Jo. It's obvious I'm not cut out for this. I'm sorry your dad flaked on you for this adventure, and I'm even more sorry I'm about to do the same thing."

There it is.

She's finally said it.

It's like a kick to the gut, hearing her say the words I've been dreading. Partly because I don't want to quit. Partly because I do. But mostly, because I think she *is* cut out for this, or at least she could be. When Dad bailed, he broke so much more than our family. He broke Mom. He broke me. He broke *everything*. Ever since he shut the door on our family, the two of us have been fumbling along, trying to figure out this new kind of life. But we're failing. I'm failing.

Mom starts to cry. I plunk down on the ground beside her. It's too hot for touching, but I push my shoe up next to hers and press a little bit, to remind her that I'm here. We're in this together, but I can feel her slipping away. I refuse to let Mom think she's not tough enough for this. I *know* she is—or at least she used to be—and I *think* I am.

I need us to finish.

"We can do this," I tell her, since it's all I can think to say.

"I'm sure *you* could," Mom says, sniffling. I glance over at her and realize I actually can't believe it's taken her this long to cry. I'd been expecting a lot more tears, but she's made it much longer than she'd thought she would without crying. She blubbers on, "You're a tough cookie, and I bet if you were out here with your dad, you'd be just fine. But I'm not mentally tough enough to take this kind of torture. It was a mistake to even try. I'm sorry I let you down. You don't deserve that."

"No," I say, shaking my head. "It's not a mistake. I don't want to be out here with Dad. I want to be out here with you. And we *can* finish. We just need to keep walking." I scramble to my feet and grab my pack, but I grab it wrong—too quickly and too carelessly—and it knocks against my leg, and I fall. My knee twists angrily as I hit the ground. The pack lands on top of me, pinning me down. I scream from the pain, even though it doesn't hurt as much as my blister did this morning. But if I can't cry, then I need to scream, and right now it's Mom's turn to cry. I shove my pack off to the side and try to straighten my knee, scraping it across loose rocks as I twist it back into a more natural position. My leg is covered in dust and dirt, my knee is throbbing, and now Mom's tears are falling on me and turning all that dirt into soupy mud.

"Oh, baby," Mom says, and starts crying harder. "I'm sorry."

"It's not your fault," I choke out. "I'm the moron who fell."

"You're not a moron," Mom says. Then she starts to laugh through her tears. "But you did fall, and I don't even know how that *happened*. I feel like I was watching it in slow motion, but I couldn't do anything to help, and I'm so sorry . . ." She's almost choking now, she's laughing so hard.

But she's also still crying. ". . . I don't mean to laugh, but it was just such a silly way to fall."

"Wow," I say, glaring at her. "Thanks?"

"We've been hauling these packs up and over boulders all day, and there are so many roots across the trail to catch your foot on, and so many places we've climbed on this hike where there is *actual* risk of falling or tripping. But you just tripped on your own two feet." She snorts out another laugh, and a big bubble of snot comes out of her nose.

Now I'm laughing, too. "My knee really hurts," I tell her. "And I didn't trip. My pack knocked me over."

Mom snorts again and leans over to inspect the scrape on my knee through her tears. She gives my leg a pat in a way that tells me it won't need stitches and will probably be okay—eventually. Then she swipes at her tears, streaking her face with mud and snot and even more filth. A moment later, she rolls onto her hands and knees, and starts to push herself back up to standing. She holds out a hand, and I let her help me up, too. I test my knee; it's sore, but I can still put some weight on it. "You okay?" she asks.

"Yeah. You?"

"Yeah." She nods. "Should we keep walking?"

I give her a look. "Are you sure?"

"No," she says. "Not sure at all. But I'll try. For you."

"And for you," I remind her.

"You're right," Mom agrees, slinging her pack onto her shoulders. She manages a small smile. "For you *and* me."

# CHAPTER TEN
# BEAR LAKE (MINUS THE BEAR, I HOPE)

We're two miles shy of Bear Lake—somewhere around nine and a half miles into our day—when we get to a campsite where we could potentially stop for the night. I stare at the trail ahead continuing to slope upward. It feels like we've been climbing uphill for the past five miles straight.

I look over at Mom to see if she might be thinking what I'm thinking.

It's so tempting to call it quits for the day.

It seems like it's already getting dark even though it's only about five o'clock, and there is nothing less appealing to me than climbing another two miles today. Not even a swim is worth that kind of torture. We reach the spur trail leading into the campsite, and Mom and I decide we might as well take a look. I know what "take a look" means: We're probably going to stop here unless there's, like, a family of bears and a full-blown hornet's nest that have already claimed this spot as their own.

I'm relieved. Today has been tough in more ways than one, and I'm ready to be done for the night. My knee hurts so much that I'm kind of limping, and my blister seems to have spread to the entire back of my foot. But when we hike into the campsite, it's immediately clear there's no water to be found. We pull out the guidebook and see that this is one of the campsites that's listed as having a water source that's "unreliable in dry conditions." Very helpful, guidebook. Very helpful.

"So . . . we trudge on?" Mom asks me.

I didn't realize how much of a relief it would be to have *Mom* finally be the one to suggest we trudge on . . . until it happens. I need the push, even though our water bottles have been teetering dangerously close to empty for the past hour, so we really have no *choice* but to move on. Unless we want to turn into raisins. Or shriveled heads on nub-bodies. "We trudge on," I agree. "It's only a couple more miles, right?"

To show my gratitude, I ask if I can lead for a while and then I start walking back to the main trail. We drag along in more silence for the next half mile or so, and pass a few groups of people who are heading back to their cars after a day of hiking.

"Gorgeous day for a walk!" one says with a friendly wave, leaping and jumping over rocks like a mountain goat as she heads back down the hill.

"Oof, that pack looks heavy!" another guy says, laughing. "Good for you."

I don't wave or laugh. Both my arms and my mouth have lost the ability to function, and Mom and I exchange a look that says, "How dare they be so annoyingly *jolly* around us right now?"

We come to yet another ridge, and down below, I can see a sparkling lake off in the distance, through the trees. It's set deep in the valley between this mountain and the next, tucked into the forest like a magnificent blue jewel. I follow the trail along the ridgeline, and just a bit farther along we come to a perfect overlook where we can stop to admire the lake. I slough off my pack and creep as close to the edge as I dare. "I'm pretty sure this is Bean Lake," I tell Mom. Bean and Bear Lakes are partners, two lakes that create a sort of infinity symbol shape if you were viewing them from over-head or on a map, nestled together side by side, deep in the woods.

The sinking sun's rays strike the lake in a way that makes the water look like it's glittering with diamonds. All those bursts of golden oranges and buttery yellows and deep, magical blues and pinks uncover a smile I didn't think I had in me. We've had stunning views of Lake Superior at various points over the past few days, but this lake is something different. It's like we uncovered a secret, a hidden lake that only reveals itself if you're willing to put in the time and effort to walk here.

"This *almost* makes today's hike worth it," Mom says quietly, resting her chin on top of my head. "Am I Bear or Bean?"

"You're Bean. Definitely," I say.

Mom smiles. "Yeah."

We snap a couple selfies with Mom's phone, and then she insists on taking a few pictures of me alone since she says she looks "like something a cat threw up." Then we keep walking, eager to get to a place where we can take off our shoes and wash our bodies. Thankfully, the next mile of trail leading to Bear Lake is flat. We walk the ridge that follows one edge of Bean Lake, way up high, then we pass through some trees and come to the far end of Bear Lake.

When we finally get to the campsite, there are at least five tents that I can see, along with a few hammocks scattered around a giant dirt-crusted area.

"Hey, hey!" an older woman cries, raising her hand in a wave to greet us. She looks like a grandma and appears to be traveling alone. She's sitting in a little camp chair next to a tiny tent, only big enough for one, eating something that looks like beans and rice straight out of a small, metal pot.

"Is this the Bear Lake campsite?" Mom asks, scanning the area.

"Well, the official site is down the hill," the woman tells us, pointing in the general direction of the lake. Her hair is wet, and she's wearing a pair of soft pants with little lobsters on them. "But both the tent pads are full down there, so I wouldn't bother hauling all your stuff down just to have to hike back up again. We've got plenty of room for you to join us up here."

"Is this an official Superior Hiking Trail site?" Mom asks, her voice barely a whisper. One big thing I know about Mom: It's probably a teacher thing, but she's *not* a rule-breaker. There are designated campsites all along the trail that are considered "official." Then there are places that people sometimes set up camp for the night that are *not* official or approved. We've seen a few of these "stealth camp" spots as we've hiked, and Mom always *tsks* when she can see evidence of someone having camped somewhere they're not supposed to. The real sites along the trail all have latrines, and campfire rings, and a little wooden sign that tells you the name of your home-for-the-night.

"Not *officially*," the woman tells us. "But there are only a couple tent pads down by the lake, and this is a popular section to hike, so I've heard both of them usually fill up by noon most days. A lot of people just set up camp here where there's a little more room."

I swivel my head to watch Mom's reaction to this. She immediately starts shaking her head. "I don't stealth camp," she says slowly. "I can't do it. Jo, we need to keep walking."

The woman laughs and gestures around at all the other tents already set up for the night. "This isn't exactly stealthy," she says. "It's more like overflow camping."

I don't really know what our other options are at this point. I'm pretty certain neither of us can make it another step, and it's going to be dark soon besides. If there isn't room for us down at the official site by the lake, there isn't room. But we have to sleep somewhere tonight.

Mom shakes her head again. "It's against the rules."

"Would it make you feel better to know there's a latrine up here?" the woman asks. "And a fire pit. So even if it's not listed in the guidebook as an official site, it's official *enough* that they gave us toilet and fire facilities."

Mom throws her pack onto the ground. "That's good enough for me."

"Oh, thank God," I say, throwing my arms into the air. "I actually thought you were going to make me keep walking." As I say it, I realize Mom was *willing* to keep walking, even if it was just to avoid breaking the rules. That says something. That she didn't start crying again *also* says something.

We find a flat-ish spot that fits our tent and set up quickly. Then we toss our stuff inside, change into Crocs, grab our water pump and bottles, and head for the lake. Dinner and reading will need to wait; swimming can't. The trail down to the lake is treacherous, and I'm glad I'm not trying to navigate it with my pack on my back at the end of an eleven-and-a-half-mile day. But I'm also excited when I realize that this rocky descent is a lot easier than it would have been for me a few days ago. I'm getting better at this trail thing.

At the bottom of the hill, we follow a path along the lake's edge to the "official" Bear Lake campsite. There are a couple of weeny tents set up right near the shore of the lake, and that's about all there's room for. There's a medium-size soft-looking dog on a long leash, sound asleep next to one of the tents. It doesn't even lift its head to greet us as we pass. It's very pretty down here at the lake's edge, and I'd give anything to spend another night with a pup, but there definitely would not have been enough room for us to sleep down here, too. The official site is, in fact, totally full.

I point to an area full of big boulders a little farther along the lake's edge. "That looks like a good spot to jump in," I say. We put our Crocs in "adventure mode" so they don't fall off, then wade into the lake with all our clothes still on. My mom doesn't even stop to check for leeches, which I decide not to mention. But it tells me she's gotten better at trail life, too.

"This is amazing," I say, floating on my back in the water, with my legs and arms all stretched out like a starfish. I stare up at the sky, which is dotted with pink-and-cream clouds, and think about absolutely nothing. After the day's stress and emotional battles, my head feels like it's crammed full of ramen, a useless lump of salty noodles. The only thing I'm able to process is how good the water feels cradling every one of my aches and pains.

The sun has nearly sunk below the ridge on the west side of the lake by the time we climb out of the water. Mom and I pull off our shirts and pants and wring them out. I give the pits of my T-shirt a quick sniff, to make sure the swim did its job. Then we perch on a rock, letting the air dry our skin and undies and sports bras while we filter water, filling our bottles and our bellies with the crisp, cool lake. The silence takes over, and for once I decide that I actually kind of like it. This is not a lonely silence; it's a comfortable, *relieved* silence. I stealthily watch my mom squeeze our filter bag and take long, slow sips of fresh, cold water. She tilts her face up to the sky and smiles, and I feel myself relax a little more.

"Mrs. Conlan?" The sound of someone calling Mom's teacher name is so unexpected that, at first, I assume my noodle-brain is imagining it. "Sarah Conlan, is that you?"

Mom turns on her rock. "Julia?" she calls out. She glances down at her camp swimsuit, and hastily pulls her soaking wet T-shirt over her body as she stands up. "What on earth are you doing here?" She starts laughing, heading toward the woman who's now picking her way across the rocks to reach us.

"Same as you," Julia says, opening her arms to give Mom a hug. She's very tall, maybe even taller than Mom, and her dark hair is all twisted into a dozen braids and wrapped up under a soft pink bandanna. She's wearing glasses and carrying a paperback book in one hand; it looks like sci-fi, based on my quick glance at the cover. She smiles at me over Mom's shoulder and adds, "Wow. Is that Jo?"

I flash her a quick wave. "Yep."

"Wow," Julia says again. "She wasn't even around when I had you for fifth grade, and now she's, like, a full person."

Aha. Mystery solved. Former student.

Mom turns to me and says, "Jo, Julia was one of my favorite students ever. I had her in my class, what . . . ?" She looks at Julia and says, "Fifteen years ago?"

"That's probably about right," Julia agrees. "I'm twenty-six now."

"Are you teaching?" Mom asks, and my instinct is to zone out. We bump into a lot of Mom's former students, so I've heard this conversation play out a thousand times. When I was little, it used to annoy me, the way her attention could be so quickly drawn away from me and onto another kid. But now I kind of like watching her interact with old students.

All of Mom's students seem to feel connected to her, no matter how much time has passed. Watching them light up when they bump into her, and seeing how excited they are to tell her what they're up to now, proves what I always knew deep down: Mom is a great teacher. She's had hundreds of students in her classroom over the years, but she seems to remember all of them. And she's genuinely interested in hearing what they've been up to since the last time she saw them. I always knew she was a great mom, but to know she's generally a great *person* making a difference in the world? That makes me love her even more.

I've only had a handful of teachers I'd be excited to bump into in the real world: Mrs. P, my first-grade teacher, was cool and gave really good hugs. And then there's

Lauren, our middle school's library volunteer. Our district can't afford media teachers for the middle schools, but we have a couple parents and college kids who come in a couple times during the week to help with book checkouts. Lauren and I have the exact same taste in books, so she helped me find some really good new-to-me ones last year in sixth grade.

Mom and Julia continue their conversation, and I tune in just in time to hear that Julia is a fourth-grade teacher in Iowa, and she and her girlfriend are spending their summer hiking before school starts up again. They're doing a full thru-hike of the Superior Hiking Trail, and they're going northbound, just like us. "Maddie's a photographer, so she's been taking pictures along the way. We're taking it slow," Julia says. "We usually shoot for about ten miles a day, so we have time to enjoy our evenings and can stop to let Maddie do her thing during the day." She suddenly stands up. "Come meet her and our dog, Murphy. We're set up on the edge of the lake, right over there."

I'm a little annoyed with Julia for pulling Mom and me out of our silence, even if she does have a dog. I slip my T-shirt over my head, but don't bother wearing my wet pants. My underwear looks enough like a swimsuit, I reason, that I can get away with no pants for a while longer. Mom seems to come to the same conclusion, since we both grab our pants and follow Julia around the edge of the lake in sopping shirts and bare legs.

Maddie is as tiny and pale as Julia is tall and dark. She's curled up inside a hammock that's hanging right along the lakeside, and at first, I don't even notice her in there. But when Julia tells her she has someone for her to meet, Maddie's head pops out of the hammock fabric, looking almost exactly like a baby bird in a nest, waiting for food. "Hi," she chirps. "I'm Maddie."

After we get all the introductions out of the way, and I spend some time petting and hugging Murphy, Maddie and Julia invite us to bring our dinner down and eat with them at the lakeside. Now it's my turn to be overwhelmed by all this socializing. I offer to climb back up the hill to get our stove and a lasagna—and to take a little break, knowing that Mom will be there when I get back.

As I pick my way along the lake's edge, I glance back and catch a view of my mom, head thrown back, laughing at something either Julia or Maddie has said. It feels good to see her like this, more like the mom she used to be. Maybe the trail is starting to work a little of its magic, after all.

I smile and hustle up the hill.

Day 4: Fault Line Creek to Bear Lake
Miles: 11.5 miles
Toilet Paper Count: 16 squares
Smell Factor: Full-on vile. It's like punishment to live in my own skin.
Major Pains: Stupid heat and sun are killing me!

Plus blister and bad knee. The ankle is almost normal again, maybe? But I'm a mess, so who knows.

   <u>Day's Soundtrack:</u> Old Taylor Swift songs

   <u>Injury Count:</u> Two (both mine—my blister, and a wounded knee)

# PART TWO

## BEAR LAKE

TO

## SECTION 13

(16.5 MILES)

## CHAPTER ELEVEN
# MORNING MUSH

When we wake up in the morning at Bear Lake, Mom is like a completely different person. I roll out of the tent and find her laughing and smiling as she chats with a few of the other people who were sleeping in tents or hammocks near us last night. I quickly do our morning pack-up chores—rolling our sleep mats, stuffing our sleeping bags, and breaking down the tent—so I don't disrupt whatever spell has been cast on her.

Part of me worries that her change in attitude is only temporary, a result of bumping into Julia and Maddie and getting to have dinner with friends last night. Maybe she perked up because she finally has someone other than me to chat with. But another part of me hopes something in her changed after her breakdown yesterday. Maybe those last few awful miles to Bear Lake helped her realize that she *can* do this. Whatever the reason for her mood-shift, it's like someone flipped a switch or changed her batteries overnight and she went from half dead to more than half alive.

Last night, Mom and I ate down at Julia and Maddie's

campsite—along with a couple of other people who were staying at Bear Lake for the night—listening to everyone tell stories about hikers they've met on the trail. Mom lit up while we chatted with people. She hasn't spent much time with friends the past couple of years, in part because the combo of divorce-stress and school are exhausting. That's what she tells Gram anyway, when I've overheard their conversations on the phone. But I also know it's because most of her friends are part of *couples* she and Dad used to hang out with together. Late one night while we were watching a movie, just the two of us, she confessed that it's weird to go out with any of her friends and feel like she's an awkward extra wheel. Like the whole balance of the group is off.

Luckily, because they're in between my age and Mom's age, it worked for Julia and Maddie to hang out with both of us, without me feeling like a kid tagging along at an adult party. But the very best part of last night was cuddling with Murphy, who might be the sweetest dog I've ever met. He's some kind of mutt, Maddie told me, a mix of lots of different kinds of dogs. He's sort of shaggy like a sheep, and his nose is huge and soft and black. His pointy ears stick straight up from his head but flop over at the very top. And he does this cute thing where he pulls back his lips and sort of smiles a little bit when his tail is really wagging.

After we ate, I slipped away to read along the lakeshore while Mom and Julia compared stories about teaching and another guy played a harmonica. Maddie and Murphy came over and sat beside me for a while, but Maddie didn't try to talk—we just hung out, each on our own rock by the lake, me reading and her writing. She shared her Cadbury milk chocolate bar with me, which—other than Mom taking this trip in Dad's place—is about the nicest thing anyone has done for me in months. She and Julia already feel like friends, and I really hope we see them again.

One cool thing I've started to realize about the trail, is that the people you meet out here have hundreds of different stories. Who we are in real life, and the reasons we're each on this journey, really don't really matter at the end of the day—the only important thing is that we all chose to be out here, at exactly this time, for some reason or another, and that's a big thing to have in common. I feel like that kind of connection makes you instant friends, in all the ways that matter most.

But unfortunately, even the *best* friends can't erase a sore stomach, or a busted-up knee, or feet that feel like they've been dunked in a vat of acid. So as great as Maddie and Julia and Murphy made me feel last night, my morning is still *awful*. I feel like a glob of poop that's stuck to the bottom of a shoe—smushed and stinky (even after our swim last night). My stomach hurts (again), my knee is throbbing, and my pants aren't yet dry from our swim even though I hung them over a tree limb to air out overnight.

Once I've loaded everything up, with the contents of our

entire trail lives shoved into our two packs, I plunk down next to Mom and take the mug full of cold oatmeal she offers me. My stomach clenches at the sight of it, and I almost puke when I spoon a bite into my mouth. It feels like boogers on my tongue, the bland goobers look like chunky phlegm, and that thought actually makes me gag.

"I'm not hungry," I tell my mom, passing back the cup full of oatmeal. "I can carry it out. I'm sorry." Just like toilet paper in the woods, when you're backwoods hiking, you have to pack out any food you don't eat, too. Anything we don't finish has to go in a bag that we carry, along with all our other garbage, and it gets hung at night with all our other food. Luckily, today is resupply day, so we'll be able to get rid of all our trash and leftovers later this afternoon when we meet up with Gina. Still, the thought of that cold, goobery oatmeal sitting inside my pack doesn't do my stomach any favors.

"I'll finish it for you," Mom offers, digging my dirty spoon into the bowl of cold mush. My single bite of oatmeal almost comes back up again, but I turn away and try to think about something else while she eats my discarded slop. Mom nudges me on the shoulder. "You okay?"

I can't help but smile through the nausea. It's a complete reversal from the past few days. Most mornings, after the initial shock of waking up and standing on my aching feet, I perk up and get ready to go in a hurry, before Mom has a chance to quit on me. She usually drags, and by the time we get on the trail, I've already had to give her a pep talk or two. But today, I'm pretty sure she's the one who's going to need to give *me* a pep talk. I'm going to need someone to drag me off this log and roll me down the trail. "I'm okay," I lie. "Just kind of foggy this morning."

"I know that feeling," Mom says, giving me a little side hug that feels really good, but also makes my stomach curl a little more than it already was. "Hey, it sounds like we're going to end up around the same place as Maddie and Julia again tonight," Mom tells me, lifting her eyebrows in a question. "Should we try to camp in the same site as them?"

"That would be amazing," I say, finally perking up a little. I'm tired of camping alone, just the two of us, and another night with Murphy would be a dream come true. Mom is pretty good company most of the time, but knowing we have friends who will be waiting for us at the end of the night makes me a little more willing to start. Even if we don't end up saying a word to one another, knowing friends are *there* if you need them or want some company is sometimes enough.

Suddenly, I really miss my regular-life friends. Outside of school, I haven't seen much of any of them this past year, and it's not until this exact moment that I realize that's all my fault. I've been so busy trying to figure out how to move on with our lives, to shelter both me and Mom from the Dad-shaped hole in our lives, that I haven't taken much time to pay attention to all the *other* things that have been gone. This morning, I'm really missing all the people who haven't walked out on me. But that's the good thing about great friends, I guess. Even if you're not quite yourself for a while, you know who will be there waiting for you when you're ready.

And as much as it kills me to admit this, even just to myself, I really, really miss my dad. Even though I'm mad at him, and even though I hate the way he acted, I still miss him. And that combination of emotions makes me feel even more sick to my stomach.

Mom heads up to the latrine, and while I pull on my filthy socks, I think about my last conversation with my brother before Mom and I hit the trail. He'd told me he was excited for me, and said Dad was, too. Jake said Dad told him he was really proud of me for going, even though it wasn't going to be the trip I'd been planning. It felt good hearing Dad had said that.

Even though I know he probably thinks we're going to fail.

Even though he didn't bother saying it to me directly.

Even though he isn't out here to see how great I'm doing on this hike.

Even though Dad left us, and even though he chose another family over ours, I do still care what he thinks. Maybe too much. And maybe that's why I've been trying so hard to keep a positive attitude, even when this trail is trying to kill us.

Because I don't want Dad to think I need him.

Because I *don't*.

I'm doing this hike for me. And Mom's doing it for her. To prove to ourselves—and everyone else—that no matter how many times we get knocked down, we can get up and keep walking. And if we can do this huge thing for ourselves, maybe we'll get even better at being there for each other.

Or we'll shrivel up and turn into nubs.

I shove my other foot into its sock and lace up my shoes. By the time Mom gets back from the latrine, I have my pack on my back, I've adjusted my straps, and my poles are in hand. My stomach is still rolling, my blister is screaming, and my knee is throbbing—but I'm gonna just keep walking. No matter what.

# CHAPTER TWELVE
# A NEW VIEW

The first few miles of trail after we leave Bear Lake are a serious climb. The unrelenting sun might not be beating down on us, and Mom might not be crying, but this whole day is supposed to be rough regardless (I overheard some people talking about it during dinner last night). Today, I feel like I only need to drag *myself* down the trail for once, and it's both easier and harder knowing that.

Somehow, keeping a positive outlook is easier when I know it's my job to keep us *both* going. But now that Mom seems to have perked up overnight, I only need to worry about *me* making it through the day. For some reason that makes it a little harder to stay cheery.

I can suddenly feel every twist, ache, and pinch in my body.

I let Mom lead the way, since I have to keep stopping to catch my breath. Whenever I stop, I urge her to keep going, letting me fall farther behind to get some space, since I don't want her to see me dry heaving into the ferns that line the edge of the trail. There's nothing in my stomach to puke up, but it would feel great to just barf and get this feeling out of me. I know I didn't eat anything weird, since we've been eating pretty much the exact same things every day we've been out here. But my stomach feels like the inside of a washing machine, churning and tossing around and around.

Mom forces me to have a protein bar about an hour into our hike, even though I insist I'm not hungry. "Breakfast is the most important meal of the day," she says.

"Not mine," I grumble. "My most important meal is ramen, and second most important is dessert."

"Those are your *favorites*," Mom clarifies. "But favorite and important are different things."

I bite tiny pieces off the bar, hoping my stomach doesn't revolt. By the time I'm halfway through the bar, I do feel a little better. But I'm not telling Mom she was right.

A little over an hour into our hike, we come to the bottom of a huge, daunting climb. The path is just jagged rocks and roots, and our arms and hiking poles have to do almost as much of the work pushing our bodies up the hill as our legs and butts do.

"I can't do it," I tell Mom, my voice barely a whisper. "Today, I actually think I might die if I have to get up this thing."

Mom stops, turns around. "You *can* do it. In fact, you *have* done plenty of climbs just like this dozens of times already, and you will again."

I nod, but I'm pretty sure she's wrong. My legs feel like

bags of sand as I drag them up step by step. As we climb, I notice that I can hear my own heart beating in my chest.

*Da-dud.*

*Da-dud.*

*Da-dud.*

The pounding echoes through my body, thudding in rhythm with each step and poke of a pole. I can almost make out the distinct beat of each chamber of my heart thudding inside my ears. I pay closer attention, trying to feel the blood moving through my body. Hearing and feeling my heart beating, pushing me up this hill, reminds me that I am still very much alive. Even after everything that's happened the past couple years, my body still knows how to survive. *I* know how to survive. Sometimes it does feel like the world—and this trail—are out to get me, but I've got this. I take another step.

*I've got this.*

*I've got this.*

*I've got this.*

"Hey, Mom?" I say when I can see the top.

"Yeah?" she pants back.

"I didn't die. Just FYI. It looks like I have survived to climb yet another mountain on this evil trail."

She laughs. "Good to know."

The path levels out and we approach a massive rock jutting out over the stunning valley below. We drop our packs and walk out onto the rocky ledge. Mom sits, and I join her, both of us gazing out over a tiny beaver pond below. Stands of jagged pine trees and ribbons of untouched wilderness stretch out for miles in every direction. A hawk flies past, right at our level, and I swear I can hear the swoosh of its wings in the wind.

"This is okay," Mom says softly, after we've rested for a while. "I mean, I've seen *better* views, but I guess this is fine?"

I laugh. "Meh."

"Mediocre," Mom adds.

I shrug. "So-so."

Now Mom is giggling, too. "Only all right."

"Ho-hum," I say in an Eeyore voice.

"Gorgeous," Mom says, ending the game. "This is absolutely unbelievable. Worth every step to get here."

I turn and narrow my eyes at her. "Was it, though? Worth *every* step? I feel like I could have cut this morning's climb in half, and still feel like we deserve this view."

"Fair enough," Mom agrees. After a long pause, she adds, "I love doing this with you, Jo. This isn't an adventure I ever would have thought I'd want to do, and I can safely say there isn't anyone I'd want to be out here with other than you, but you make it worth it." *Uh-oh*, her tears are back. "I just wanted you to know that."

"Ditto," I say. I wait for her tears to dry in the wind, then I add, "But can we make one deal, moving forward?"

"What's that?" she asks.

"After this trip, can we please not have oatmeal ever again in our lives?"

# CHAPTER THIRTEEN
# THE DRAINPIPE

"So . . . should we climb down this beast of a hill one at a time?" Mom asks, leaning against her poles for support. We stand side by side, staring down the edge of what appears to be a sheer drop-off. "Or stick together?"

"I can't do this alone," I blurt out, and it's the absolute truth. "Definitely together."

She takes a big breath. "What's the strategy here? Hiking poles on, or off?"

"I'm butt-scooting," I tell her, pulling my pole straps off my wrists. "There's no way I'll keep my balance going down this if I'm standing up."

When I checked my map to look over today's route this morning, I noticed something labeled "The Drainpipe" a few miles before the parking lot where we're meeting Gina to get our resupply box. There are several points along the Superior Hiking Trail that have been given fun names. My favorite of these is "Mediocre Overlook." Could there be anything *less* tempting and *more* curiosity inducing than an overlook with that name? Whose job is it to name these trail bits anyway?

Usually, these odd names on the map amount to nothing special. Just a cute label on a wooden sign that leads to a spur trail or overlook that might be worth noticing.

But as soon as we reach Tettegouche State Park, it's obvious the Drainpipe *is* something special—and not in a good way. From what I can see, this section of the trail looks to be a treacherous, nearly straight-down wall of jagged rocks. There are no handrails, no ropes, no safety measures at all to keep a person from rolling right off the edge to her death below. It looks like some sort of rock giant had a morning like mine and threw up the entire rocky contents of its stomach into the middle of a leafy forest.

"I guess I'll take my poles off, too," Mom says, pulling her own straps off her wrists. She traps both of her poles in her left hand. Neither of us has moved any closer to the edge of the drop-off. We both stand firmly on solid ground, right before the trail dips down into nothingness. We've climbed up and down plenty of steep sections of the trail this past week, but those were like a gentle river ride compared to this death-roller coaster of doom.

I'm completely and totally terrified. I take a deep breath, and say, "Will you go first?"

Mom puts one hand on the ground and carefully scrambles down the first natural stair, and then awkwardly eases herself to sitting to slide one more level down. If she weren't right there in front of me, several rocks down the cliff, I wouldn't have seen what happened next. But because all my attention is focused on the space directly in front of me, I watch as one of Mom's poles slips out of her hand and plinks onto a rock below. It bounces, twists, then continues to spiral and fall—straight into the open mouth of the Drainpipe. Silently, we watch in horror as her pole bounces from boulder to boulder, getting farther and farther away from us, before it finally comes to a clattering stop in a nest of enormous rocks, hundreds of feet below us.

"Oh. My. God," Mom says, her voice just a breath.

"That could have been me," I say, which probably isn't what either of us needs to hear right now. "That could have been my body bouncing down the rocks like that."

"But it wasn't," she says.

"Not yet," I add. "I haven't started down yet."

"It *wasn't* and it *won't* be." Mom sits down on a giant rock and drops her head in her hands. "This is insane. There has got to be an easier way to get down this mountain."

"At least we're not hiking south on the trail, or we'd have to climb *up* this beast," I say.

"Fair enough," Mom says. Then she continues the long and careful process of scooching down the rocky embankment on her butt. I trail close behind her, careful not to get *too* close so I might bump into her, but also close enough that I can follow her butt-path down each section of the cliff. My breath is shallow. I can't look down to the bottom, or I know I'll freak out. I focus on taking it one rock at a time.

I'm sure we look ridiculous scooting and bumping and slithering down the rocky steps with our heavy packs strapped on our backs, and it takes us nearly fifteen minutes to get down, but we finally reach the bottom.

By some kind of miracle, Mom's fallen pole has landed near enough the trail that she's able to get to it without putting herself into any further danger. As soon as we're safe on solid, lower ground, we sit at the bottom of the Drainpipe, thanking our lucky stars that we're still alive. And in one piece.

That's when Julia, Maddie, and Murphy come hopping and skipping down the rocky Drainpipe trail, making it look like the wall of rocks that nearly killed me and my mom a few minutes ago is nothing more than a gentle gravel road. "Hey, guys!" Maddie calls out, waving to us as she bounces from foot to foot down the rocks. Murphy's leash is attached to a belt around her waist, so her hands can be free.

"How are they moving so fast down that cliff?" Mom mutters. I start to laugh, thinking about how embarrassing it would have been if they'd showed up fifteen minutes earlier. Just in time to watch us sliding down the hill on our butts, terrified for our lives, when they're making it seem like this treacherous rock wall is just another pleasant morning walk in the woods.

"How's your day going so far?" Maddie asks, stepping lightly toward us. They're already down. Less than two minutes, and they're at the bottom. Murphy lies down at my feet while Maddie grabs a water bottle out of the side pocket of her pack and takes a swig of something pink and sort of fizzy looking. "That's a pretty crazy hill, huh?" She doesn't wait for us to answer before yammering on, "Do you two want to trek with us the rest of today?"

In some small ways, I don't. I've started to enjoy the solitude of the trail during each day, where I can practice being alone without *actually* being alone. But in other, bigger ways, walking with someone other than just Mom might be kind of nice. And after seeing what a couple hours with them did for her last night, I suspect my mom might kind of like the chance to walk with Maddie and Julia, rather than just me. "Yeah," I say. "That would be great."

# CHAPTER FOURTEEN
## TRAIL ANGEL

Apparently, Maddie and Julia don't need a rest after conquering the Drainpipe, because they're looking at us like they're ready to get a move on. Mom hobbles to standing and gets her pack secured. Then she and Julia set off together at the front of our group while Maddie, Murphy, and I lag behind.

"So, Jo, huh?" Maddie asks from her position up ahead of me on the trail. "Is that short for anything?"

"Josephine," I tell her, speaking louder than normal, since I've discovered it can be hard for the person in front to hear what the person walking behind is saying. The trail's only wide enough for one body, so we almost never get to walk side by side. "But I've always just been Jo. My mom is a big fan of the book *Little Women*, and I was born in March. I'm named after the character Jo March."

"Oh my gosh!" Maddie says, her tiny voice reminding me so much of a bird that I wonder if maybe she has a pair of fairy wings hiding under her backpack. "I love that!"

"Yeah," I say. "Only problem is, I've tried to read *Little*

*Women* like twenty times, and I just can't drag myself through it. I'm more of a *Hobbit* and Harry Potter kind of girl."

Maddie laughs. "I'm not a big reader, period," she says. "So I get that."

"What?" I gasp. "What do you do at night on the trail if you're not a reader?" I've never understood people who say they're not readers. I always want to dig through my shelves and hand them something I just *know* they'll love so I can try to change their mind. I think I get that little hobby from my mom, whose classroom is filled with all kinds of books for her students: graphic novels, *Calvin and Hobbes* comics, silly chapter books, realistic fiction, adventure stories, and my personal favorite: fantasy.

"I write, mostly," Maddie says. "Just notes about our day and stuff, but I almost always start to zone out while I'm writing and then I end up just sitting and thinking. I don't usually get a ton of chances to sit and think in my regular life, so I kind of love being bored out here. But some nights we play cards. Do you and your mom play pinochle?"

"No," I tell her. "My dad and brother and I used to play a lot of board games, but we've never been much of a card family."

"Wanna learn?" Maddie asks. "Julia and I are sick of playing war and solitaire, so it would be awesome if we could turn you into pinochle partners and play a four-person game."

"Sure," I say. Luckily, we're hiking on a flat section of the trail right now as we wind through Tettegouche State Park. Mom and I don't ever talk this much while we walk. It's hard to chat, watch where you're stepping, and breathe all at the same time.

"How'd you and your mom end up out here together?" Maddie asks. "Dad and brother not interested in hiking?"

*Ugh.* I guess it's my own fault that she's asking about them. I shouldn't have mentioned Dad and Jake at all, since now it's opened the door for Maddie to ask questions.

I suddenly think back to the summer before fourth grade, when the three of us—me, Dad, and Jake—made it our personal goal to hike seventy-five miles of new-to-us trails around Minneapolis during the summer. A combo of our three ages at the time. Sometimes, our neighbors would let us borrow their dogs to hike with us. Almost always, we would stop for ice cream on the way home. A few times, when our hikes took longer than we had planned, we'd meet up with Mom near the end and she'd bring a picnic dinner for us all to eat outside by Minnehaha Falls or on a comfy bench along the Mississippi River.

Mom would always use the alone time while we were all hiking to try to get through the teetering stack of books she kept piled up next to the couch, or to clean the house, or she'd meet up with friends for a coffee. Lots of times, Dad would grab Mom's hand and jokingly try to pull her up to come along with us, but she almost never did.

Is that part of the reason Dad left, I wonder? Because Mom

never hiked with us? That's a pretty stupid reason to abandon your family. But *any* reason would be better than no reason, which is as much as I have now.

I'd give anything to understand *why*.

What made Catherine better than Mom? What makes Ellie more deserving of Dad's time this summer than me? What could we have done differently to keep my dad from walking away from everything I love so much?

"They both love hiking," I say, so quietly that I wonder if Maddie will hear me.

"It's pretty cool that your mom's the one out here with you, though," she says. "Neither of my parents ever would have done a trip like this with me. I was kind of a city girl until I met Julia."

"How long have you two been together?" I ask, hoping this is an easy way for us to shift the topic away from my family and onto hers.

"A little more than six years," she tells me. After a little pause, she asks, "Are your parents still together, Jo? I wouldn't normally ask that, but I got the impression from your mom last night that maybe things have been a little . . . rough the past couple years?"

"They're divorced," I say, realizing it's easier to talk to someone who's not looking you straight in the eye. "My dad left for another family. He moved in with his girlfriend and her kids before his and Mom's divorce was even final." I'm surprised I'm able to spill these details to

Maddie—whose back is to me as we walk down the trail—that I haven't told anyone else the past few years. All my friends' parents are still married or have been divorced for as long as I've known them, so it's hard to talk to any of them about this stuff. My mom signed us both up for therapy sessions after Dad left, but I really hated going and talking about my feelings with a stranger and so she let me stop—"temporarily."

Maddie whistles. "Oof," she says. "I totally know what you're going through."

"You do?" I ask.

"One hundred percent," she says, her voice still all chipper and cheerful, even though we're not even talking about anything happy. "My parents split up when I was fifteen. I don't totally know what went *wrong*, but at the time, it was pretty easy to see that nothing was *right* anymore."

"Oh," I say, realizing she doesn't know what I'm going through. Not at all. Because I thought everything was fine. Learning Catherine existed was a total shock. And then I met her kids, who seemed to know my dad—or at least this *new* version of my dad—better than I did. In a matter of days, I realized everything I thought was true about my life just wasn't. "Are you still close with both of your parents?"

Maddie laughs. "It was a mess for a couple years, but yeah—now I'm probably closer to both of them than I ever was growing up."

Suddenly, we pop out of the woods onto a busy state park trail. It's wide enough that Maddie and I can walk side by side. Mom and Julia are waiting for us up ahead, so that's the end of our conversation and I'm kind of relieved. We all walk together for a while. Eventually, we get to cross an amazing swinging bridge that takes us across a big river and waterfall. We continue our trek through the park, passing all kinds of people who are out for smaller day hikes and who can't seem to resist staring at our giant packs. I feel proud when people stare, to be honest. Especially because I'm so short, I know I look pretty tough with a big turtle shell full of supplies on my back. I wish I *felt* as tough as I look.

"Our meeting spot is just up here," Mom tells me after we've climbed another steep rock, pointing straight ahead down the trail. She stops to talk to Julia and Maddie. "Do you want to pop out into the parking lot on Highway One with us? We're picking up our resupply box from my college friend, Gina, and knowing her, she'll have some extra treats for us in the car. Whatever she's got, we'd be happy to share."

"One thousand percent yes!" Maddie shrieks, like a little kid at an amusement park. Murphy picks up on her excitement and starts barking—big, round *woof*s that echo through the forest around us. He and Maddie bound ahead, leading the way to the parking lot spur trail.

When we reach the parking lot—which is only a couple hundred yards off the main Superior Hiking Trail—Gina is there waiting for us. She starts waving wildly, arms over her head, as though we might not see the only person standing in the middle of the gravel parking lot. "You're here!" she cries out, rushing toward us. She's carrying a box of ice cream sandwiches, has a big plastic bag from Subway draped over one arm, and I can see a cooler full of red Gatorade and sodas sitting open beside her car. Gina is my hero.

Mom runs forward, embracing her friend in a giant hug. We just saw her five days ago, when she dropped us off at our starting point on day one, so it feels a little dramatic that they're *so* excited to be together again. But in regular life, Mom and Gina haven't actually gotten to see much of each other since the divorce and I know Mom wishes it were different. Gina's one of Mom's few single friends, but she lives a couple hours north of Minneapolis, so she's just not near enough for them to hang out as much as I think either Mom or Gina would like.

As soon as they split apart, Maddie runs forward and gives Gina a hug, which takes Mom's friend by surprise—at first. Then she hugs Maddie back and says, "Hey there, stranger. I'm Regina." Even though Gina has one of the thickest Minnesota accents I've ever heard, she grew up in Tennessee, and she still has a little Southern twang that sneaks out sometimes. I love it and wish I could copy it.

"Regina, honey, you're our trail angel," Maddie responds in a similarly faint Southern accent, squeezing her tighter. I wonder if maybe Maddie grew up somewhere other than

**105**

Minnesota, or if she's just really good at copying accents. I hope I remember to ask later.

I'm fascinated, watching this interaction and insta-hug between Regina and Maddie. Before Mom and I came out here on the trail, it would have seemed crazy to me that one little act of kindness like a cold drink and a sandwich could connect two people so quickly. But I think back to how happy I was about that shared Cadbury chocolate bar last night, and realize how grateful Maddie must feel to be a part of this surprise feast. And that sort of kindness has made her and Regina instant friends, just like it made me and Maddie instant friends.

Maybe there's a reason Maddie and Julia landed at camp with us last night; for the past few years it's felt like me and Mom are totally alone, but I'm starting to realize there's this whole community of people ready to hold us up and help us out when we need a boost. We just need to let them.

While they hug, Murphy noses his snout into the Subway bag. Gina pulls it up and away just in time. I wink at him, since I will *totally* share some of the meat and cheese from my sandwich with good ol' Murphy just as soon as I have a sub in my hand. He deserves every kindness, too. Maddie pulls back and says, "Oh, and by the way, I'm Maddie, this little cutie is Murphy, and the taller cutie over there is Julia."

"I'm glad I brought enough food and cold drinks to feed a small army," Gina says, passing out Gatorades and sodas from the cooler. I watch Julia and Gina exchange a hug, and see Mom smile as she passes drinks to everyone. I can tell she's excited we get to share her friend and our feast with the people who boosted her up today. Gina waves us toward the shade at the side of the parking lot and says, "Help yourselves to everything. I have sandwiches, and drinks, and some apples and carrot sticks. We can sort through your resupply box in a bit, Sarah. But first, hand me your phone so I can start charging it, and then start talking since I can't wait to hear everything!" She bustles around the car, setting up chargers and helping us all take our packs off. Then she orders, "Y'all better dig in quick, before the ice cream melts."

I don't need anyone to tell me twice. I grab a ham sandwich for Murphy, and an ice cream sandwich for myself, then sit down in the middle of the parking lot, relaxing in the beautiful shade cast by Gina's car.

<u>Day 5: Bear Lake to Kennedy Creek</u>
<u>Miles Today</u>: 10
<u>Total Trail Miles</u>: 49 (almost halfway!!)
<u>Toilet Paper Count</u>: 24 squares (good thing we got more in the resupply box, because I'm pretty sure Mom's been using more than her fair share... The old roll was almost gone!)

<u>Smell Factor</u>: I can't even smell myself anymore, so I guess that's good?

<u>Major Pains</u>: Stomach, feet, hip bones. Pretty much everything hurt today.

<u>Day's Soundtrack</u>: A jewelry store radio ad jingle! Total torture.

<u>Injury Count</u>: Three (all me)—my knee, and now TWO blisters (one heel, one big toe). How is this fair???

# CHAPTER FIFTEEN
# BEAR FOR BREAKFAST

I wake up feeling much better than I did yesterday. But my body still hurts, and I have a feeling that climbing up to Section 13 today isn't going to help with the aches and pains. Apparently, Section 13 is a popular place for people to go rock climbing, which just tells me there's gonna be a lot of uphill ahead of us. And after yesterday's Drainpipe, I'm even more nervous about today's steep uphill climb. I just hope my legs hold out.

Last night, we slept down in this sort of murky valley, camped along a dried-up creek. The site itself is pretty, but without any water in the creek, we don't have anywhere to fill up our bottles for today's hike. Mom never wants to start our day without two full liters each and I guess this makes sense, for safety's sake. But every liter of water weighs more than two pounds, so some days I'd honestly rather risk it than carry too much.

Luckily, Julia heard there's a lake down a secret trail, less than half a mile from our campsite. So while Mom drinks her coffee and Maddie and Murphy loaf around in the tent a little longer, I offer to join Julia on a water-hunting mission. It feels amazing to set out from camp without my pack. It's almost like I have a bouquet of helium balloons attached to my arms, I'm so light and airy and springy.

"Hey, how many miles total have you gone now?" Julia asks as we turn down the side trail toward this mystery lake. I really hope it's not a beaver pond. Beaver ponds are often pretty, but they're totally still "lakes" that are created when a beaver stops the water that *had* been flowing to another destination by building a dam or lodge. So the water often ends up kind of green and algae covered, and it definitely wouldn't win a taste war with yummy river water.

"Funny you should ask. I just added it up last night! We're at forty-nine—almost halfway." Until now, I'd been keeping track of our trip just day by day. But it suddenly felt like the grand total might be a big enough number that I wouldn't be discouraged when I added up all days together. Almost halfway is pretty good, but it means we have at least this many miles (and more) left to hike.

"Whoa," Julia says, sounding impressed, even though I know they'd already hiked close to one hundred miles of the trail before we met up with them at Bear Lake.

Our trail spills out at the lake, and it looks like maybe it's part of some sort of camp or something, since there's a cute little dock and a few boats on the other side. It feels a little like we're trespassing on land that isn't meant for us to use.

Quietly, we take turns dipping our filter bags into the lake and as soon as everything's full, we turn and head back. Once we're back on the trail to our campsite, Julia asks, "How are you feeling about the hike so far?"

"Some days, fine. Other days, less than fine," I admit.

"But 'fine' is the best it gets?" Julia laughs.

"Fine is a stretch," I tell her. "The hiking part is horrible. I'm just here for the pretty views and chocolate." This isn't true, but it's as much as I want to say.

Julia laughs again. "I'm impressed. It's not easy, what you're doing."

"Also, I'm doing it for bragging rights," I add, suddenly feeling bad for the lie before. She and Maddie have been nothing but kind to us, and I owe her at least a piece of the truth. "I want to be able to hold it over my dad and brother that we hiked farther than they did when they came out here on the same trip when Jake was my age."

"Those are all super-noble goals," Julia tells me, pushing aside a branch that's sloped across the trail. Just as I step under it, I sense movement in the woods to our right.

We're not alone.

We've just turned back onto the main Superior Hiking Trail, and we're probably about a quarter mile from our campsite. I peer into the thick cover of trees lining the edge of the trail, but can't see anything.

Some mornings, I'm more on edge than others. Just like at home, ever since Dad left us for his new life, there are bad days and good days. Times when I can ignore all the stuff going on around me and pretend everything's fine, good, *great*. Then there are the times when all I think about are the *what-ifs*.

What if I could have done something differently, to make Dad stay?

What if I had been at the company picnic that day, and been stung by a bee, and dragged Dad out of there before he ever met Catherine in the first place?

What if something happens to Mom and I have to live with Dad and his new family full time, forever?

What if Mom's miserable for the rest of her life?

Out here, there are times when I manage to forget we're in Mother Nature's hands, and I get to pretend this whole adventure is nothing more than a pretty walk in the woods with my mom. But there are plenty of jittery times, too, when I let myself think about all the dangers that surround us. And that's when I remember what I've stepped over many times the past couple days, what I'd failed to process on our morning walk to water: bear scat.

Tentatively, I take another step forward, all my senses on high alert. I don't smell anything strange, can't see farther than a few feet into the deep woods on each side of me, and don't hear anything—until I do. It's a sort of huffing sound, almost like the sound of a quiet clap, coming from the thick trees beside the trail.

A branch snaps. Then another.

Julia freezes in front of me, and I almost crash into her before I stumble into the space by her side.

Off the trail to our right, the branches overhead begin to shake. There's another crack, then a crackle, and it sounds a little like twenty humans are crashing through the woods all at once. It feels like time shifts into fast-forward, as suddenly a giant black bear spills onto the trail less than five feet in front of us. It gracefully bounds across the trail, stopping to look at us.

As soon as we realize what it is, Julia screams. And I mean *screams*. Her body practically melts into the ground as she backs up and falls in on herself, trying to create as much space as possible between her and the bear. Her water bag rolls to the side of the trail, like a forgotten water balloon at the end of a party.

Meanwhile, I begin to sing—loudly.

The books I read taught me that a black bear *might* be scared off by loud noises; pounding a pan, or making yourself seem big and scary, or creating a lot of noise will likely frighten it away. But there are a lot of *exceptions* to that rule: if you—the human—are somehow unlucky enough to be standing between a mama bear and her cub. Or if it's a grizzly bear. Or if the bear is just not in a great mood that day and it thinks you might have food it wants. Which means it's a risk to be standing there and singing, for sure, but it's kind of my only option. Especially since Julia is now crying and has rolled into a ball.

The only song that comes to mind in that second is "Yellow Submarine" by the Beatles, and so I yodel that out at the top of my lungs. The bear studies me. In reality, it probably lasts for less than two seconds. But it feels like an hour.

Finally, the bear bounds back into the forest, heading off in the other direction.

For the next minute, I continue to sing: "WE ALL LIVE IN A YELLOW SUBMARINE, A YELLOW SUBMARINE, A YELLOW SUBMARINE!" as Julia whimpers and hugs her legs to her chest, moaning.

"That was a bear," she whispers.

"Thank you, Captain Obvious," I say, since this is pretty much the perfect moment for that name.

"And I totally freaked out," she squeaks.

"You did," I say, cringing.

"Jo . . . did you just sing the Beatles to a black bear?" She gazes up at me from her curled-up position on the ground.

"I did," I nod. And then I realize: I just sang to scare away a bear.

While the adult beside me rolled up like a pill bug and panicked, *I* dealt with it. Me. Alone. "I think I might be some kind of bear whisperer . . ." I murmur.

"Is it gone?" she asks, her face lined with worry. She collects her water bag from the underbrush along the side of the trail and checks to make sure it didn't get punctured in the fall.

I listen to see if I can hear any more branches cracking in the woods, but it's quiet. "I think so."

"Whoa," Julia says as she stands up and brushes off her pants. "That is *not* how I planned to react to my first bear encounter. You cannot tell Maddie I freaked out like that, okay?"

I laugh and hold out my hand for a fist bump. "Deal." Then I remember Mom's vow that she'd quit if we saw a bear. I don't want to quit. We're almost halfway there now, and I suddenly just *know* we're gonna make it. "As long as you don't tell my mom we even *saw* a bear. This morning's adventure is going to stay our little secret."

# CHAPTER SIXTEEN
## SECTION 13

"Meat slice?" Mom offers. We got a giant summer sausage in our resupply package yesterday, and it's already pretty much gone. Neither Mom nor I want pasta again tonight, since it's still so hot out, which means we're making tonight's dinner out of tortillas and sausage slices. We also got some dried mango in the resupply package, but I already ate it all.

Mom and I are sitting out on this massive rock outcrop we found that looks out over the world below. I hold out my hand and Mom uses her Swiss Army knife to slice a piece of summer sausage into my grubby palm. I motion for her to keep it coming, and when I have three fat slices in a stack, I line them up and wrap them in a tortilla like a cold burrito. I dig back into my book as I eat.

Getting a new book was the best part of our resupply box. I traded out my super-battered copy of *The Hobbit* for a paperback copy of *Harry Potter and the Half-Blood Prince*. I've read it at least a dozen times—and I know most people probably wouldn't choose this one as their favorite in the series—but it's the Harry Potter book with the most scenes I want to read over and over. I convinced Mom to let me put *two* books in our next resupply box, arguing that I'd be stronger by then and should be able to carry a little more weight. Which means that in a few days I'll get to trade out Harry for *Amulet* and *Breadcrumbs*.

Tonight at Section 13, we're camping with Julia, Maddie, and Murphy; a woman who's around my mom's age and is hiking the whole trail southbound alone with her dog (she's already tucked into her tent for the night, I think, and it's only six o' clock); and two couples who are on a single-night overnight hike together and heard this area has great views.

They heard right. The climb up to Section 13 wasn't a treat, but it was worth it. It's like you're standing on top of the world up at the top of this cliff, with unbelievable views out over the golden and green valleys below. Somehow, even with the steep climb, today ended up being a pretty easy hiking day, since we only went about six and a half miles total. It's crazy to think that six and a half miles feels like "not much" now, since a week ago, the idea of hiking six miles in a day would have horrified me. But when you have the whole day ahead of you with nothing planned except hiking six miles, it feels like luxury.

We got to camp after the lady and her dog, but before all the other people got to camp for the night. Which meant we had a huge choice of spots to put up our tent, and Mom and I found this sort of tucked-away nook on top of a hill, just above the main fire pit area. We're surrounded by cozy trees, we have a pretty direct path to the latrine, and it feels like we're wrapped inside our own private forest. With our evening chores done (we had to collect water a mile or so before we got to our site, since this is currently marked as a dry camp, due the lack of rain this summer), we have nothing to do but look out over the world below.

"Check it out," Mom says, pointing. "An eagle."

The views from the Section 13 cliffs are almost impossibly vast. This high up, you can see everything—inland lakes, tiny beaver ponds, cleared logging areas, and miles and miles of trees. But the sky is the wildest thing; it's endless. Sitting in my camp chair, perched on the edge of these massive cliffs, I feel a little like a tiny speck inside a snow globe. The sky is everywhere, surrounding us on every side.

I peer into the openness and see what Mom's pointing to—a soaring bald eagle, dipping and swerving in the wind. We watch as it traces lazy circles across the sky, cutting a twisting path through the pink-and-blue evening.

"When I was a kid," Mom tells me, "eagles were an endangered species, and it was rare to spot one in the wild. Their population is growing now, so I know it's not a big deal, but it's still exciting when I see one like this."

"It's pretty cool," I agree. The eagle soars closer to our perch on the rocky cliff, and I'm able to get a better sense of its size. This bird is massive. "I'm glad I'm not a small dog or a very tiny hobbit," I say. "Or I'd be worried it would swing by and grab me in its talons for dinner. Or take me as its human prisoner, feeding me only grubs and worms until I learned the way of eagles."

"Yes," Mom says, chuckling. "It's a good thing you're not a small dog or a tiny hobbit."

"Hold on to the meat stick," I remind her. "If that eagle comes any closer and nabs it, we're back to eating pasta for dinner."

"Okay, Jo." Mom laughs.

She's in a good mood again. It's so great hanging out with my mom when she's cheerful and back to her old self. I forgot how much fun she can be, since so much of the past couple years have been icky. I still wonder if maybe, probably, this hike is finally beginning to work its magic on her.

Does she feel stronger?

Proud that she's leading me on this incredible adventure?

Is she starting to forgive Dad . . . the way I kind of wish I could?

"Mom?" I ask, tentatively.

"Yeah?" she says, her eyes following the eagle's path through the sky.

"What happened between you and Dad?"

**119**

There's a long pause, and I wonder if maybe she didn't hear my question. Maybe my words got carried away with the wind. "I really don't want to talk about it, Jo," she says finally. "I'm sorry."

"But I do," I say, hoping she realizes that just by *asking* the question, by pressing past her *I'm sorry*, I'm telling her how much I *do* want to talk about it. It's been pretty much radio silence in my house, ever since the big announcement that our-family-as-I-knew-it was done. I'm not one to push; I'm usually more of a listener. But as hard as I've listened, I still don't know as much as I want to know. As much as I *need* to know.

Mom turns her short little fold-up chair so she's facing me. "Okay," she says. "What do you want to know?"

I have so many things I've been longing to ask, but at the moment, the only thing that comes to mind is: "Why? Why did he do what he did? Why did he pick Catherine and Ellie and Sam over us?"

She sighs. It's a big sigh, the kind with a big exhale at the end. Her frustrated-teacher sigh. "I honestly don't know," she says eventually. "It's hard to fully understand why other people do what they do."

"So you just . . . *don't know*?" I say, not believing it for a second.

"You're asking a big question. It's complicated," she says, which is probably just as annoying of an answer as "I don't know."

"I can handle complicated," I tell her.

"Jo . . ." Mom says, trailing off again.

It's a war of silence, and I have every intention of winning this one. I'm not backing down or giving her an out. I need to understand what really happened, why Dad made the choices he made, so I can decide how much I'm supposed to hate him. Finally, Mom says, "I'm going to be more honest with you than I probably should be." She raises her eyebrows, as if asking me a question. If she wants to know if I'm cool with honesty, the answer is *yes*. I nod, telling her to continue.

Mom fiddles with the Swiss Army knife in her hand, flicking a blade in and out, in and out. "Things were not great between us for years. It's not that we fought, or hated each other, or . . ." She pauses again, then starts up mid-sentence. ". . . We were more like roommates or coworkers than we were husband and wife." She looks at me, checking to see if I want her to go on, so I nod again. "I guess I'd never considered divorce an option for me, so I never imagined the possibility of splitting up. But your dad, I guess he wanted more."

I want to ask her so many things: Did he even try to fix it with you, or did he just take off? How long had things been like that, and why didn't *I* ever notice? Were things bad before Catherine, or only after she showed up? But I don't ask anything, because I don't want to interrupt Mom and make her stop talking.

"Maybe, over the years, I forgot what it was like to

actually be in love," Mom says after another huge sigh. "Maybe your dad didn't, and that's why he went looking for it again." She stops suddenly, as if she's just remembered she's talking to me and worries maybe she's said too much. She hasn't.

"I'm not lying when I say there are things I don't totally know either, Jo," she continues. "It really *is* complicated. It's hard to not place blame, but you have to try to avoid that."

"Oh no," I say, shaking my head. "I can see exactly who's to blame here."

"But you *can't*, that's the thing," Mom says. "It's not a simple situation, and there's not a simple way to look at it. The important thing to remember is, your dad is your dad. And he's a great dad, regardless of what happened between us."

I start to speak up, to argue that a "great dad" wouldn't ditch the father-daughter trip he's been promising for years. But before I can say that or any of the other reasons he doesn't seem like a "great dad" to me, Mom blurts, "He hasn't been as great *lately*, but he's juggling a lot right now, too. He's still trying to figure it out, and he's going to get stuff wrong sometimes. Just like I will. Divorce isn't easy on anyone."

I squeeze my lips into a tight line. "Sometimes I hate him," I tell her.

She releases a third huge sigh. "Sometimes I do, too," she admits. "But I don't want to."

"I don't either," I agree.

"And hard as it is for me to say this to you," Mom says, "we have to figure out how to forgive and move on. Even if I don't like the way he handled everything, I do think we're better off apart. I really do. Much as I hate that you and Jake are wrapped up in our whole mess, I have begun to realize that both your dad and I will eventually be better parents and better people apart than we ever could have been together. And you'll be better off if you let him back into your life, Jojo."

"What if he forgets about me?" I ask softly. "I mean, he has this great new life now, and I'm part of the old one, and—"

Mom cuts me off. "He will *never* forget about you. Both of us love you so, so much, Jo. It's been a hard, terrible, strange couple of years, and Dad knows how angry you are with him—rightfully so—so he's been trying to give you space. But he'll always be your dad, and I hope you can work things out together."

Now it's my turn to sigh.

"I do think an important part of healing from this kind of thing is forgiveness," she tells me, in what I've come to know is her teacher voice. "I hope you can start to forgive him, so you guys can begin to move forward."

"Are you going to forgive him, too?" I ask.

She laughs, then cringes. "I'm not quite there yet," she tells me. It's a much more honest answer than I would have expected. It isn't a mom-answer; it's a friend-answer, and I appreciate it. "I think I'm finally getting past the shock and anger. I'm trying to work on the acceptance piece of healing.

I think I'm almost there. Then I hope I can move on to forgiveness. But it's going to take me a bit longer to get there, I'm afraid."

I nod. "That makes sense."

Mom runs a hand through her mess of hair and closes her eyes. "I'm sorry we haven't talked about this before."

"It's okay," I tell her. "I'm glad we have now."

"Me, too," Mom says. Then she stands up and scoots her chair over so it's touching mine, so we can sit side by side and look out over the darkening quilt of sky and forest together. "You know, I kind of feel like I won the lottery by getting to go on this trip with you. You sure are one tough cookie. I love that we're doing this together."

"Yeah," I say, resting my head on her shoulder. "Me, too."

"But maybe next time," Mom whispers, "we could do a girls' trip to a spa in Hawaii instead?"

<u>Day 6</u>: Kennedy Creek to Section 13
<u>Miles Today</u>: 6.5
<u>TOTAL Trail Miles</u>: 55.5

<u>Toilet Paper Count</u>: I give up. Counting squares every time I pee is getting old. We made it five days on one roll, so we should be good until our next resupply box.

<u>Smell Factor</u>: The pig barn at the State Fair smells better than the inside of our tent does each night.

<u>Major Pains</u>: All the same stuff. Luckily, nothing new to add today!

<u>Day's Soundtrack</u>: "The Imperial March" from *Star Wars*

# CHAPTER SEVENTEEN
# LATRINE OF DOOM

I wake up to the sound of someone screaming. It's that half-light, dawn time of morning, so it's hard to tell through the tent fabric if it's *super* early, or just early. I roll over and notice that Mom's sleeping bag is empty beside me.

My whole body freezes. I'm pretty sure my heart actually stops for a second.

Someone is screaming.

Mom's not here.

There it is again, another scream and then a loud swear. I hear the zip of a tent, and the swish of someone kicking off their sleeping bag somewhere else in the campsite. This launches me into action. I scramble out of my own bag and crawl to the door of our tent. I tug at the zipper too hard and get it stuck in the fabric. I back it up, and try again, this time managing to get the screen door open enough to crawl into the vestibule and tug open the rain fly. My legs carry me down the little hill toward the fire pit area—the spot where Julia, Maddie, Murphy, and the other woman and her dog set up camp last night. The other two couples set up their tents in a little spur campsite down another hill from where we're all staying.

We all exchange bleary-eyed, confused looks. "Mom," I finally say, since it's now very much evident who screamed, based on who's not standing there.

"Sarah!" Julia calls out, her voice booming through the campsite.

"Here!" I hear my mom call out from somewhere in the woods, in the direction of the latrine. We all run toward her voice, jumping over jutting tent stakes and jagged rocks, scanning the woods for her. The latrine is pretty far from camp at this site, in a wooded section of the forest that felt private and relaxing when I used it before the sun went down last night. But now that I'm in a hurry and in the half-light of dawn, I realize that the trail heading back to the latrine is slanted, and I feel myself slipping and sliding as I race through the woods.

We find Mom sprawled on the ground near the big brown latrine, clutching her leg and wincing, in obvious pain.

"I fell," she says, squeezing her eyes closed.

I notice that our roll of toilet paper has unfurled itself down a hill nearby, leaving a pitiful trail of white from the latrine into a pile of damp-looking leaves. My mom is clutching the empty plastic baggie we keep our TP and sanitizer in. For one brief, horrible moment, I'm more worried about the fact that we no longer have toilet paper than I am about my mom's injury.

I snap my eyes back to Mom, just in time to see Murphy give her a big, sloppy kiss on the ear. Mom snorts, but it sounds less like laughter and more like pain. "What happened?" Julia asks. "What hurts?"

"I was putting our toilet paper back in the bag and I guess I must have stepped off trail," Mom said. "My leg slid, and when I tried to catch myself from falling, I did something to the other ankle." She tries to sit up, but it's clear that even moving her leg causes extreme pain.

"Which ankle?" Maddie asks.

Mom points to her left foot. The woman we don't know crouches down to inspect it. She gently touches the knobby outer ankle bone through Mom's sock. Mom winces again, sucking in a quick breath.

"It could be broken," the woman says.

"Are you a doctor?" I ask.

"Heart surgeon," the woman says, and the rest of us exchange a quick, surprised look. "It could just be a bad sprain, but you're going to want to get it looked at."

"Can you stand up?" I say, shooting *please, please, please* vibes in Mom's direction. "Let me help you." I reach out a hand and Mom takes it, letting me attempt to pull her off the ground. But as soon as she puts weight on her left leg, she crumples to the ground again.

Eventually, with help from both Julia and the heart surgeon,

Mom manages to stand. She wraps an arm around each of them. Together, they awkwardly shuffle back toward camp with Mom hopping along on only her right leg. Maddie, Murphy, and I shuffle along behind them while I gather up the trail of soaking wet toilet paper, so we don't leave a trace. "This is not good," I mutter to Maddie.

She smiles feebly and says, "Maybe it will be okay."

Back at camp, Mom settles into her camp chair near the fire pit and elevates her leg on one of the camp's wooden benches. I quickly heat some water for instant coffee and make Mom a cup that I bring to her along with a breakfast bar. She takes both and gives me a look I instantly recognize: This is not going to be okay. "I'm sorry," Mom says.

"Why are you sorry?" I ask. "No one *chooses* to fall on the ground that close to a latrine. And it must have been a bad fall if you dropped the last of our toilet paper." I reach out to touch her ankle and can see that it's already a bit swollen. "Does it really hurt? Do you want me to take off your shoe?"

"It really hurts," Mom says sadly. "I'm leaving the shoe on, since I'm pretty sure I won't ever get it on again if I take it off."

Before I can ask what's going to happen next, Julia plops down on the bench next to Mom's foot and says, "The good news is, we're not that far from a road. The bad news is, to get there we're going to have to backtrack the last mile or so we climbed up yesterday afternoon."

I don't know what I was thinking would happen, but as soon as Julia says this, it hits me: We're done. This is it. We didn't make it one hundred miles. We didn't even make it to our second resupply stop. We failed.

"Do you think you can make it?" Julia asks, but we all know that Mom doesn't really have a choice. It's not like we can leave her up here to turn into a wilted nub, and she obviously can't continue on as planned. The end of our climb yesterday was almost entirely uphill and very rocky. I don't know how Mom's going to get down that, but she also doesn't have much of a choice. If we moved farther down the trail, it would be miles before we passed another road. Heading back to Lake County Road Six is the fastest and only option to get the help she needs.

Once it's clear what needs to happen, the plan comes together quickly. We decide to leave Julia and Maddie's tent set up with their gear and packs stored inside it, so we can focus most of our energy on getting Mom help, as quickly as possible. Maddie helps me pack up our tent and stuff our gear into our packs, making sure I have super-easy access to a few essentials that will get us through the day: the water filter, all our remaining drinking water, some quick and easy snacks, Mom's cell phone, our paper maps, and the emergency credit card. After we get safely back to civilization, Julia and Maddie will hike back to gather their own stuff before they move on up the trail.

The heart surgeon helps to wrap Mom's ankle using a smooth stick for stability and an extra sock as a sort of ACE bandage thing. Once that's set, Julia and Maddie thank her and tell the doctor she's free to set out ahead of us, which she only agrees to once the other two promise they'll accompany me and Mom to get help.

Maddie and I carry the packs and handle Murphy's leash, as always, while Julia takes on the task of helping Mom walk. For once, carrying a heavy pack seems like the preferable option. Mom can't put *any* weight on her left leg, so Julia ends up pretty much carrying her down the trail. It takes us almost four hours to make it down from the Section 13 campsite to the parking lot, but we do finally make it and are relieved to see a couple just climbing out of their car to set out on a day hike.

"Hey!" Maddie calls, running toward them at full speed, as if they might disappear if she doesn't reach them quickly enough. She throws Mom's pack on the ground and wiggles her arms in the air. "We need a ride! She's hurt."

The couple look our way, and Mom waves. We take a few minutes to explain what happened. The couple immediately agrees to drive us to the nearest town, where Mom plans to get in touch with her friend Regina to come pick her up and bring her to a doctor. "This is why the hiking community is the best," Maddie says, high-fiving the couple. "We're totally ruining your hike this afternoon, and you're totally okay with it."

The woman—who is somewhere in her mid-fifties or maybe sixty-something—reminds me of my elementary school librarian. They have the same hair, and her face is friendly. The man—who kind of looks like a younger version of Gandalf in the newest *Hobbit* movie, because they have the same beard—pats Maddie's shoulder and says, "The trail will still be there tomorrow, and now that I'm retired, I've got all the time in the world."

The nice older couple starts loading our packs into the back of their hatchback. That's when it fully hits me that we're done. We've reached the end of our trail, and who knows when or if Mom will ever be willing or able to come back to finish this hike with me. I can feel the tears coming, and I know I can't stop them from falling, so I dig my face into Murphy's fur and let him lick the wetness off my cheeks so no one will see me crying.

I can't believe we failed.

I have to go home and tell Dad that he was right; we *couldn't* do it.

I was actually starting to feel like we might make it—no, I *knew* we were going to make it—but once again, I'm wrong about everything I thought I knew to be true.

When I stand up, Maddie pulls me in for a hug. Mom is already loaded into the backseat of the car and Julia is leaning in to talk to her through an open window. I open the other door and sit down, hoping the stench from my clothes and body don't transfer to the nice backseat fabric of the couple's car. There are no wrappers or crumb-filled plates or crumpled-up homework papers in their backseat, like there always are in our car. My hiking shoes have already left a brown streak on the clean floor mat.

"Jo?" Julia says through the window as the older couple settles into their spots in the front seat.

I blink and smile, then open my mouth to thank them for their help. But before I can say anything, Maddie crams her head in beside Julia's and says, "Come with us."

"Why?" I ask. "Did I leave something at the trailhead?" I don't want to get up. My legs have started to do the thing they do at the end of each day of the hike, where it almost feels like they're draining. All the fear and worry and work and disappointment of the morning have started to leak out of my pores. My body is like a bike tire that someone has poked a tiny hole in, and all the air is slowly leaking out as I sink deeper into the strange but comfortable backseat and the fact that we're done.

"Hike with us," Julia adds. "Finish what you started. We're going the same way as you, and there's no reason you need to quit just because your mom got hurt."

I look from Maddie, to Julia, to my mom. Mom is nodding. "I don't want to ruin this for you," she says. "Please finish."

"I can't," I say, knowing it's true. I ask the first question that pops into my head. "Where would I sleep?"

"In your tent," Maddie says. "You can borrow Murph if it makes you feel more comfortable than staying in a tent alone."

"I'm not going to leave my mom when she's hurt," I say, thinking about all the times these past few years when Mom and I have stuck together—kept each other safe—after Dad disappeared. I can't abandon her now, not right when she needs me most.

"What are you going to do if you come with me?" Mom asks. "Are you going to hold my hand while I get an X-ray? Drive me to the hospital?"

"I don't drive," I say, knowing that makes me sound like an idiot. She obviously knows that. "And I'm not allowed to be in the X-ray room because of the radiation."

"Precisely," Mom says. "Gina will be more than happy to take care of me, and I can come along to deliver your next resupply box in a couple days. You can take the next few days of hiking to decide if you want to finish. If you want to be done when we come with the next food box, we'll bail you out."

"But—" I begin, then realize I don't know what else to say. It's not like I can say what I'm really thinking, which is that I'm too scared to do this alone. I'm not strong or brave enough. I'll be too likely to quit if Mom's not right there, urging me along. Bottom line: I can't.

I know I can't.

"You can do this," Mom says, almost as if she can hear my thoughts. "Please. Or the guilt will kill me. Don't let me blame myself for ruining this for you. I refuse to let a latrine injury be the thing that stands between you and reaching your goal."

I choke out a laugh. "The latrine of doom," I say.

"Please," Mom says again. "Go with Maddie and Julia.

They offered to do this, and I trust them completely. I know you can handle it. Please don't quit because of me."

It would be so easy to quit. To go in the car with Mom, take care of her, make sure her ankle is going to be okay. I have the perfect excuse to be done, without guilt. But I don't want to be a quitter. I don't want to be like Dad, who gave up and moved on as soon as there was an easier and better option.

Maybe I *can* finish this.

Maybe I *do* have what it takes to keep going.

Maybe I'm not a quitter.

Maybe I'm strong enough.

Maybe . . . I can do this alone.

"Okay," I finally say, though I can't seem to get my mouth to smile. "Yeah, okay. I'm gonna finish for us."

# PART THREE

## SECTION 13

TO

## LUTSEN

(55.5 MILES)

# CHAPTER EIGHTEEN
## ALONE

Dad left us on a Thursday.

I remember, because Mom always stays late at school one Thursday a month, so she can go to the parent-teacher meeting in the evening. Most teachers don't go to those meetings, but Mom always says that she's a parent first, teacher second. So, she goes to the PTO meetings as a parent but usually gets stuck talking about stuff and answering questions as a teacher.

She always comes home from the meetings all fired up, since our school district doesn't have enough money for all the things that our school needs, and Mom says the meetings end up being a whole bunch of people complaining about stuff that none of the teachers even have any control over. I don't know why she keeps going, but she does, and that's how I know it was a Thursday.

On Thursdays, Dad and I always used to go out for pizza together—it was him, me, and Jake for a long time and then it was a date for just the two of us, after Jake left for college.

But that particular Thursday night, Dad didn't come home. I waited, snacking on popcorn and apples, until I finally caved and put a Costco mini pizza in the oven. They're tiny, so I knew I'd still be able to eat real pizza with Dad when he got home from work.

But Dad didn't come home from work. Not that night, or any other nights after that. He claims he forgot it was a PTO-meeting Thursday, and that he didn't mean to ditch me on pizza night, but I'm not sure I believe him.

Later, I found out he'd come home earlier in the day while I was at school to pack up a couple bags full of clothes and stuff. But by eavesdropping on my mom's phone conversations with Regina, I found out Dad had been slowly moving stuff into his girlfriend's house for a few weeks. So even though he didn't leave for good until that Thursday, he'd already been half out the door long before that and I hadn't even seen it coming.

It took me a while to realize that the first Thursday Dad didn't come home was the last time I was comfortable being at home alone. It was the last time *alone* didn't terrify me. That night I watched old episodes of *Survivor*, and eventually ate a second mini pizza, and by the time Mom got home I had finished off the last of the ice cream in the freezer. "Where's your dad?" she asked, thumbing through the mail I'd left on the kitchen table.

"Dunno," I said.

"I'm going to take a quick shower," Mom said, heading

upstairs. "Can you text him and find out when he's going to be home? My phone's dead."

It turned out Dad had been trying to get in touch with Mom all day, but her phone was dead. Which is how I got to be the first one to find out Dad was gone for good. He's not much of a phone chatter under normal circumstances, so let's just say that when he called me after I texted him that night, it was an extremely awkward conversation. "Jo?" he'd said, sounding surprised, as if it wasn't normal for his daughter to be wondering where he was on pizza night and as if *he* wasn't the one who'd called *me*.

"When will you be home?" I asked, half watching *Survivor* and half listening to him.

"Um . . . Jo?"

"Yeah?" I settled deeper into the couch, accidentally dropping the phone between two pillows for a second or two.

When I picked it back up, he was saying, "—not coming home tonight . . ." Then he trailed off.

"What?" I asked.

"Where's your mom?" he'd asked. Something about the tone of his voice suddenly made me feel gross.

"She was at the PTO meeting," I answered. Dad hadn't actually said anything major at that point, but there was something about the *way* he was talking to me that made me feel sick. "And now she's in the shower."

"Jo, I'm not coming home." He delivered each word like a grenade, pulling the pin and rolling those explosive words

**141**

between us, knowing it was too late to take it back and that everything was about to blow up. "We really need to talk. But first, I need to talk to your mom."

When I reminded him it was pizza night—since *pizza night* was obviously the most important thing he'd bailed on—he promised to make it up to me and suggested we go out *every* Thursday after that for pizza. But I had no interest in sitting across the table from him, pretending I still liked him.

He ruined everything: pizza night, my mom, our family. And me.

As I hike back up toward Section 13 this afternoon, I'm tucked safely and snugly into the space between Julia, our leader, and Maddie and Murphy, who generally prefer to lag behind. I'm not alone yet, but I will be tonight. Alone in my tent, with nothing but my own thoughts to break up the silence. I've avoided this exact thing for the past two years, since being alone always reminds me too much of that night my dad left. Alone, stupidly waiting for someone who would never come. Waiting, not realizing my world had already collapsed.

When we get back to camp, after a second day in a row of climbing the sharp trail leading up to Section 13, I pull the tent and stakes out of my pack and get to work setting up my bed for the night. We left all of Mom's stuff and her pack with her, but I took the tent, the stakes, my sleeping bag and pad. I'm going to share a stove with Julia and Maddie, so I don't need to carry that on my own, and they're going to help haul some of my food. The big bonus is that Mom let me take her e-reader, which is packed with a ton of books—not many that I want to read, but there are a few on there that look interesting and at least now I have more variety of reading material to choose from. My pack is heavier, now that I'm not splitting the gear load with Mom, but I'm stronger now than I was the first day and the extra weight doesn't bother me too much.

I crawl into our—*my*—tent to change out of my day clothes and into my at-camp comfy outfit, spreading all my stuff out to fill the space where Mom's sleeping bag should be. It stinks inside the tent, and this time I know it's only *my* socks that are to blame. Mom's socks aren't in here anymore, so any stink is mine and mine alone. This is not reassuring.

I pull off my sweaty clothes and socks, then lay inside my now-solo tent in just a damp sports bra and underwear. My sticky skin clings uncomfortably to the fabric of my sleeping bag, but I don't have the energy to pull on my cleanish sleep pants or my nighttime T-shirt to create a barrier. I lift one leg straight up into the air to stretch my hamstrings, and that's when I notice a wood tick buried in my ankle skin. It must have crawled into my sock and spent the day moving in and getting comfy tucked into my skin.

"Great," I mutter, digging the medical kit out of my pack. I open the small, zippered bag too quickly, and everything spills out onto the floor of the tent—bandages, various pill packets, anti-itch cream, allergy stuff, a pack of waterproof matches, and the tweezers.

I want to cry, but there's a tick in my leg and if I cry the tears are going to make pulling it out nearly impossible since I won't be able to see clearly. I haven't done this on my own yet—Mom's always been the one on tick duty—but now that she's gone, I don't have much of a choice. I refuse to be the helpless kid who runs to her new chaperones crying about a bug stuck in her leg. There's no reason I *can't* remove it, except that I don't want to. I don't want to remove it, but more importantly, I *really* don't want a tick sucking my blood for the next week out here on the trail because I'm too much of a chicken to get rid of it.

One of my friends once found a big, swollen tick on her dog a week after they'd gone on a hike, and she showed me a picture of what it looked like when they finally pulled it off his body. I almost barfed. It turns out, if a tick sticks around long enough to drink a bunch of your blood, it grows fatter and fatter until it eventually looks like a rotten grape dangling off your skin. Nope. No thanks.

I close my eyes, bite the inside of my cheek to keep the tears from falling, grab tweezers, and focus on my leg. Carefully, I position the pointed tweezer ends at the tick's body and grip it as near the head as I possibly can. You have to try to get the whole thing out all in one tug, and not leave its teeth inside your skin, or the bite spot can get irritated or infected. This tick is pretty big, so I know it's not a deer tick. Deer ticks are tiny—sometimes almost impossible to spot unless you're looking carefully—and they can carry Lyme disease. Wood ticks can also pass on diseases, but it's more rare, and usually not an issue if you get the tick out early.

Slowly, gently, I grip the tick's strangely solid body with the tweezers and tug. It hasn't dug into my skin very deeply yet, and there isn't even a mark where I pull it out. I clamber out of my tent and flick a match to burn the tip of my tweezers and ignite the tick's body, so the little bugger won't just turn around and crawl back into my tent.

I can't resist a small smile. I feel bad for killing it, but more importantly, I feel proud that I took care of the problem on my own.

See tick . . . check.

Remove tick . . . check.

Dispose of tick . . . check.

Survive the whole thing without anyone's help . . . check.

"Okay, good," I breathe out, not even a little bit self-conscious about the fact that I'm talking to myself. I'm also still mostly naked and am getting chilly in the cooling evening air. Luckily, I set up my tent in the same spot Mom and I had slept the previous night, so it feels familiar. I'm sort of secluded, and there's a tree-line shield between me and the main part of camp where Julia and Maddie are staying for the second night in a row. I climb back inside the tent and get dressed in my nighttime clothes, then survey my home for the night. "Comfy," I say out loud, hoping the words will make me believe what I'm not sure is true. "You've got this, Jo."

I slip on my long-sleeved shirt, exit the tent, and grab my food bag, trying to decide if it's a pesto and chicken kind of night, or if I'm just going to slam down a tortilla with peanut butter and call it good. I don't want either. I don't want to eat alone, I don't want to sleep alone, I don't even know if I want to be here anymore.

There's no one sitting at the fire pit when I head to the center of our campsite, so I assume Maddie and Julia are probably sitting on the rocky overlook where Mom and I shared dinner together the night before. They'd told me they might head down there to enjoy the sunset. I don't want to disrupt them, and anyway, I'm too lazy to walk down the trail to find them and the water heater, so I coat a tortilla in gobs of peanut butter and roll it up. It's gone in four bites. I finish drinking my second-to-last bottle of water, tie my bear bag to a tree where Julia and Maddie will see it and be able to figure out I've gone to bed for the night, then head for the latrine so I can get a final pee in before dark.

As I make my way back to camp to tuck in, I spot one lone piece of toilet paper fluttering in the branch of a bush just down the slope off the latrine trail. I decide to leave it there, even though I know I'm not supposed to. It's like a little flag marking the end of Mom's portion of the hike. From now on, it's just me. Alone.

"Alone," I say aloud, hoping that the more I say it, the less scary the word will sound. "Alone. I am alone, and it's okay. Alone, alone, alone. Aloooooooone." It doesn't work.

I crawl into my tent and cry myself to sleep, hoping that maybe tomorrow morning everything will feel better.

Day 7: Section 13...to Section 13 (again)
Miles: -1.3+1.3=0
Injury Count: Jo = 3 (knee & blisters); Mom = 1 (but it's a big one, so in this case 1 > 3)

# CHAPTER NINETEEN
# EGGO LAKE

I do feel better in the morning, but only by a little bit.

I'm less sad, but that may be because I'm too focused on how thirsty I am, or how I desperately need to pee, or the aches and blisters that I'd sort of forgotten about yesterday that are back in full force. Moaning, I pull off my sleep clothes and tug on my still-damp-from-yesterday's-sweat sports bra, the same filthy socks, and a somewhat fresh pair of underwear. I quickly pack up my sleeping bag and pad, stuff them and all my other gear into my pack, and then put on my T-shirt and hiking pants.

As soon as I get everything packed up, I look around the inside of my tent and sigh. For a few seconds when I woke up this morning and saw the empty space next to me, I forgot about yesterday and thought maybe Mom was just out by the campfire ring, drinking her coffee. But as soon as the sleep-fog cleared, I remembered. And now that I see all my stuff lined up without her stuff beside it, it hits me again that Mom is gone. She's not just drinking coffee, or at the latrine, or up ahead of me on the trail. She's *gone*, and I'm on my own.

It's weird doing all my usual morning chores without Mom's help, but I'm proud to realize I *can*. The tent is down and stuffed into its sack quickly. My gear is loaded up and ready to go. As I lace up my shoes and head to the toilet, I remind myself that, after today, I'll be more than halfway to my final goal. That's totally doable. If I survive less than one more week, then I'll be able to say I hiked farther than Jake and Dad. I'll prove to Dad that I don't need him, and we're fine on our own. Mom and I can do anything without him. I can survive alone.

I find Julia and Maddie hanging out near the fire pit when I get back from the latrine. No other campers showed up at Section 13 last night, so it's just the three of us and Murphy at breakfast. They've already packed up their stuff, so we each grab a bar to eat while we walk and head out.

"Did you sleep okay?" Maddie asks softly as she heaves her pack onto her back and clips her straps together. She clicks Murphy's leash into place on her belt.

"Yeah," I say. "I had lots of space. No one to kick."

Julia laughs. "I bet your mom enjoyed sleeping in a bed last night. I wonder how she's doing?"

I've been trying not to wonder about that. Of *course* I want to know what's going on with her ankle, and I hope Regina was able to drive north from Duluth to pick her up and take care of her, but I know I have to focus on my own well-being now, or there's no way I'm going to make it more than a few more miles. "I wonder what she had for breakfast," I say. "I hope someone got her waffles."

Mom's favorite food is Eggo waffles, which I've been thinking about all morning, ever since I realized that today's goal is to reach a place called Egge Lake. I decide to fill the first section of the morning's trail with a story for Maddie and Julia, about the time when I was about four or five and, for Mother's Day, I set an alarm for three in the morning so I could make Mom a special breakfast. I picked the time at random, not knowing exactly what time my parents got up in the morning but guessing three was probably early enough to beat them to breakfast.

"I got up by myself in the dark," I tell them, glad to have this memory of Mom along for my first section of hike without her. "It was before dawn, but I plodded downstairs to the kitchen all alone. I popped a few Eggo waffles into the toaster, waited for them to be perfectly brown, then tried to figure out how to make them even more beautiful." The truth is, Eggo waffles are beautiful on their own, but they're also a perfect canvas for making food art.

"I'm nervous about where this is going," Maddie says from somewhere behind me, waiting for me to continue.

"There was a can of whipped cream in the fridge, so I squirted it all over them," I say, chatting on. "Then I dropped a whole container of blueberries on top of the mound, and then sprinkled chocolate chips, pink decorating sugar, and some

M&M's on top of the whole mess." Except at the time, I didn't think it was a mess; I was sure my gift was beautiful.

The kitchen? It was not.

"My mom didn't even care that I'd destroyed the kitchen," I say, and can see Julia nodding up ahead of me. She had my mom as a teacher and knows firsthand how patient she can be. Mom's classroom is never the neatest, or the cutest, or the most organized, but it is the most comfortable and friendly class-room in the building—and that's what she cares about most.

Mom was so grateful for my Mother's Day surprise, and even more grateful when I fell back asleep in her bed, curled up next to her. My dad? He got up and cleaned the whole mess before Mom and I finally crawled out of bed again together at eight. That's the kind of guy he used to be, in the time before he only cared about himself. But now he's changed, and Mom hasn't . . . She even still loves Eggos.

I really miss her. Already, and it's been less than a day.

"I'm really in the mood for a waffle now," Maddie says, a small whine in her voice. "Or whipped cream."

Not far down the trail from camp, we come to the official Section 13 overlook. It's stunning—panoramic views of the whole valley below, and it almost feels like I've been dropped into a photograph. "This is insane," I say, plopping my pack onto the ground.

Maddie pulls out Murphy's folding water bowl to give him a drink, so we can all take a little more time to enjoy the view. If Mom were still here with me, this would totally be a photo moment. But her phone is with her back in the real world, and Maddie doesn't offer to take my picture with her fancy camera. So I try to just soak it all in, and promise myself that I'll remember this view forever.

As I gaze out at the world below, I wonder: Did Dad and Jake stop here, too? Or did they just press on, moving with focus toward their next mile marker? When Dad and Jake and I used to do day hikes together back in Minneapolis, Dad would do this thing we called "Dad Breaks." He'd hustle out ahead of us moving like a tiger-on-the-hunt through the forest, while Jake and I would sort of dawdle behind, stopping to inspect strange mushrooms or toadstools hanging off the sides of trees or to chat with squirrels. Eventually, Dad would stop somewhere along the trail and wait for us to catch up to him. But then, as soon as we'd reach him, he'd announce, "Break over," and start hiking again. He was the only one who actually got a break, but he reasoned that since my brother and I were taking little breaks along the way, we didn't really need one long one.

"Ready to keep going?" Julia asks, after we've been standing around for five or ten minutes. "Jo, how about you lead?"

I cringe. "I'd rather not."

"Okay," Julia says with a shrug.

Here's the thing I've learned: the first person walking down a trail in the morning catches all the cobwebs that spiders have spun overnight. Since no one else stayed with us at Section 13 last night, it means no one else has walked this section of trail yet today. So I'd honestly rather Julia or Maddie clear the cobwebs with one of *their* faces so I don't have to do it. It's rude, but strategic.

The rest of the day's miles are fairly relaxing. After the past few days of big climbs, it almost feels easy. We have this long stretch of trail over a marshy area, where the trail is covered with planks of wood. It's like a long dock that weaves through the wetland and over beaver ponds. We pass through sections of forest filled with trees that are hundreds of years old, then head into a logging area where all the trees have been cleared. The variety of stuff to see and the relatively flat trail make our miles pass quickly, and we make it to Egge Lake by three in the afternoon. I pick a spot to set up my tent right on the edge of the lake.

"Want some help setting up?" Maddie offers.

"I think I can do it," I say without fully thinking it through. The thought of unpacking all my stuff, and getting the tent and all the gear inside it set up for the night—alone, again? It's a lot. Yesterday, I suspect I was running on adrenaline and shock and sheer determination. Today feels like a different version of the end of day one again, and I wish someone was here to hug me and bring me an ice cream bar.

Maddie ties Murphy's long leash to a tree between my tent pad and theirs, and I'm excited he decides to curl up for his afternoon nap on a small patch of rough grass right next to my pack. His company is nice. It's not Mom, but he's a different kind of comfort. I get my tent footprint—which is a tarp-like thing that goes under the tent, that helps keep the tent itself dry and clean—set up and spread out my tent atop it. I feed in the poles and get everything hooked up so the tent is ready to go, but I don't have the energy to pump water or set up my bed area quite yet. So I leave my pack intact and toss it inside my tent, attach Murphy to his short leash, and head down to the lake's edge with my book and camp chair.

Egge Lake isn't huge, but it's beautiful. Long grass grows out of the shallow areas, and the trees crowding the shoreline are reflected in the still water, giving the whole thing a mirror effect. Little minnows dart around the rocks just out from shore. Dragonflies flit and swoop in the air around me and Murphy. I'm also pretty sure there is a pair of *swans* floating out in the middle of the lake, though they might be a figment of my imagination. I don't think swans live in Minnesota, but if I were painting this scene I think I'd *want* swans in the picture. So maybe it's my mind playing tricks on me.

I've only been reading for a few minutes when Maddie joins me lakeside, plunking down on a rock before immediately dangling her bare toes in the water. It's too chilly to swim today—I actually had to put on my not-yet-used jacket this afternoon—but I decide Maddie's is a good idea. Even if I can't wash off my whole body, I can at least rinse off my feet.

I pull my sweaty socks off and stuff them in my pocket (which I'll probably regret later) and dip my feet into the shallow lake next to hers. "Uh-oh," Maddie says as her foot moves to flick water up at me. "Oopsie."

"Really?" I say, laughing as I splash her back.

"Tidal wave!" Maddie announces, kicking her feet wildly at the surface of the water. Murphy is curious and lumbers up to investigate. As soon as he's near the lake's edge, Maddie flicks a ribbon of water up and into the air and Murphy launches himself into the lake to try to catch it. "We call this game Splash," she explains to me. "Murph loves trying to catch water like it's a ball, and doesn't ever seem to realize that there's nothing to catch. It's his favorite game, but man, he's gonna smell *awful* tonight after getting his fur all wet." Maddie side-eyes me and says, "He told me earlier today that he'd like to sleep in your tent tonight." She changes her voice so it's sort of low and goofy and says, "Please, new best friend, Jo? Can I have a sleepover with you? I like to cuddle."

I laugh and squint at the dog. "We'll see." Maddie reminds me a little bit of my brother. I realized earlier today that she and Julia are probably only a few years older than Jake is, which makes them feel more like older sisters than anything else. We're like a sisterhood out here; thinking about our group in that way makes me feel a little more comfortable and confident without my mom here.

"Stupid question maybe, but are those swans?" I ask, pointing to the big, white, majestic birds floating in the middle of the lake. "I guess even more importantly, do *you* see those two giant white birds out there, or am I inventing things? Those aren't just big ducks, right?"

"Those are swans," Maddie confirms.

"So swans are . . . real? Like, real-world real?" I ask. "I've only ever seen them at the zoo or in movies."

Maddie considers this. "You know what? I don't think I've seen swans anywhere other than those places either." She picks up her camera and begins snapping shots of the cute couple. "I've seen herons and eagles, but not swans." Suddenly, a duck floats around the bend along the lake's shoreline and Murphy goes nuts barking. The duck flaps and skim-flies across the surface of the lake. But the swans are unbothered by Murph, and continue what appears to be a slow, romantic paddle in the middle of the lake. Bright blue dragonflies dance over the surface of the water near shore. The whole scene is absolutely picture-perfect.

I hear someone else making their way down the trail into our camp. Both Maddie and I turn to see who it is. We wave at a couple who looks to be somewhere in their twenties or thirties. Neither looks happy, but they wave back feebly before dumping their overstuffed packs onto the ground.

"Are *you* going to set up the tent, or should I?" the woman snaps, less than ten seconds after they walk in.

"I can do it," the guy says back. "Just give me a sec. I have to get the mud off my shoes first."

Maddie and I exchange a look. "Mud off his shoes?" Maddie mouths to me, and I shrug.

"If you don't *want* to do the tent, just give me the stuff and I'll do it myself." I can practically hear the woman's eyes rolling from the tone of her voice.

Maddie and I exchange a quick, secretive smile. It's not nice to get joy out of someone else's misery, but these two are kind of asking for it. Even on my worst days on the trail so far, I've at least *tried* to put on a somewhat brave face around strangers. Mom and I might not have been happy or enthusiastic all the time (some days none of the time), but we tried not to spread our misery by yelling at each other.

"I don't think they're having their best day," I whisper.

"Ugh, these *bugs*," the woman says, and immediately begins spraying bug repellant all over herself and everything else within a twenty-foot radius. "John, get my back? And don't forget my neck, because this morning you forgot my neck and I got eaten alive."

"There's no room for our tent," John whines, scanning the campsite without moving his feet to actually *look* for a spot to pitch their tent. He heaves a sigh and glares at me and Maddie. "Maybe we should just move on, Angie. Find somewhere with more space and privacy."

"Are you kidding me?" the woman, Angie, growls. "What's wrong with that spot, right there?" She points to a flattish area just a few feet away from John that is very obviously a perfect place to set up a tent.

"If *you* want to lay on that tree root all night," John huffs, "be my guest."

I realize I need to put these two out of their misery before their fight escalates and this nonstop bickering continues through the evening. I think back to how chatting with Omar and Molly—and even Ben, in his silence—made me feel a little better on that rainy night back on our third day. "Where did you two hike from today?" I ask loudly, ready to reassure them it will get better, much like our campmates did for us back when we'd had that rotten day leading to Fault Line Creek. Sometimes a little kindness and reassurance from a stranger can turn a bad day into a better one.

Angie says the name of some road or trailhead, but without studying the map, I don't have any idea where it is. "How far is that?" I ask, since they seem totally exhausted and, based on their moods, I'm guessing they've probably had a long day.

"We've gone four miles so far," Angie tells me. "We started around noon."

"This is our first night on trail," John adds. "We're doing a shakedown hike to test out our gear. We're planning a thru-hike for early fall."

All the things he just said would have sounded like a foreign language to me a few months ago, but now that I've been living this trail life for over a week now, I understand that he's telling us this is the first night of a practice hike, and that they're planning to attempt to finish the whole trail at once sometime later in the year. I really hope they practice kindness toward each other, in addition to practicing hiking and using their gear, or that's gonna be a long three hundred miles together.

"My girlfriend and I are doing a thru-hike now," Maddie

tells them. "Happy to give you any pointers you need."

"We're good," Angie snaps, shutting her down without a smile. "We've done plenty of research."

"All righty," Maddie says. "If you change your mind, I'm here all night."

"No, thanks," John adds.

Angie and John go back to their bickering, while Maddie and I each laugh silently. We can hear them fumbling with the tent and poles, followed by a lot of swearing, and eventually I hear Angie scream out, "You *forgot* the toilet paper?"

"And *you* forgot dairy doesn't sit well with me," John screams back. "So all those cheese-filled dehydrated meals you bought for dinners are obviously your way of making me miserable!"

My body is shaking so hard with silent laughter that Murphy gets up from his lakeside nap spot and comes over to check on me. He snuffs his wet nose in my face, and I bury my face in his stinky neck fur just in time to stifle a snort. "Poor Angie," I say softly.

"Poor John," Maddie agrees.

"Poor us," I say, imagining Murphy adding this in his own goofy voice. But he doesn't actually say anything. He just goes back to his nap while the sound of bug spray echoes in the early evening sky.

# CHAPTER TWENTY
# SOMETHING BORROWED, SOMETHING BLUE

The temperature continues to drop, but I stick it out at the lakeside until it's almost totally dark. I have to put on all my clothes and pull my sleeping bag out to keep warm, but sunset paints the sky impossible colors of pink, then purple, then a gorgeous blue, and even though I'm cold, I just can't make myself move from the perfect spot I have set up along the shore. By the time I head for bed, Murphy's fur is almost dry, and I'm freezing, so I ask Maddie if I *can* borrow him in my tent for the night.

"For sure," she says. "That was part of the deal, right? You have a big, two-person tent and only one small person to squeeze in there. We have a two-person tent with two full-grown people and a dog that's the size of a third-grade child. It gets a little squishy in our hut with all of us packed in there."

After I hit the latrine and tie my bear-proof bag to a tree

that's a safe distance away from our tents, I nudge Murphy into my trail-house and zip us in. He doesn't seem at all concerned that he's been pawned off on me for the night and settles right into the spot next to me, falling quickly asleep.

I turn on my lantern and do a quick tick-check. Relieved to find none, I pull off a layer of clothing and climb into my bag. I notice then how much grit is floating around inside the bottom of my sleeping bag. I roll over to face Murphy and, using the dim light from my overhead lantern, study the streaks of mud and little flakes of dirt and grass and even a few small sticks that are scattered about inside our (my) tent.

I remember when all our gear was still new and fresh and clean-smelling. Back when our stuff looked like Angie and John's gear, with creases still visible in the tent fabric and that outdoor-store smell.

Some of my stuff is repurposed from Dad and Jake's hike together, all those years ago. I'm using my brother's sleeping bag. We even found some leftover dehydrated meals in their bins of hiking stuff that don't expire until, like, the year 2094.

But when Mom and I realized we were going to be doing this hike alone, together, we decided to get some of our gear fresh and new so we could put our own stamp on the whole experience. We borrowed a few things from Regina, including a lighter tent (it's a beautiful blue color, which is *far* superior to the ugly brown tent Dad used for Jake's trip), and I got to pick a backpack that fit me just right. We also borrowed a faster water heater, bought our lightweight camp chairs, found new hiking poles, and Mom chose her own sleeping bag since there was no way she was going to use Dad's.

This spring, a bunch of the families with kids in Mom's class got together and chipped in for a gift card to help us pay for everything. They gave her a gift card large enough that we even had enough money to buy the fancy bear-proof food bag so neither Mom nor I would need to figure out how to hang our food from a rope flung onto a tree every night.

I remember feeling like a complete dork in the outdoor store, holding a list of things we'd read we needed. Mom couldn't stop crying, but she claimed it was tears of joy and hope brought on by the generosity of her students' families. Eventually, a store employee found us spinning in circles and helped us figure out what we *actually* needed (bug repellent and first aid supplies) and what was on the list that could easily be left behind (including camp chairs, which we bought anyway).

Mom and I spread out everything we had collected from our big shopping spree on the living room floor as soon as we got home. We created piles of "Jo's" and "Mom's." We combined the new stuff with the stores of stuff Dad and Jake had tucked away in plastic bins and all of Regina's contributions, and then we double-checked our piles against some of the many versions of packing lists we'd found online. Seeing all our stuff spread out, filling every inch of the carpet in our living room, I couldn't believe it would all fit into two backpacks. But it did, and now most of it fits into just *one* backpack—mine.

This whole adventure—the giant packs, the seemingly endless rugged trail, the strange gear and contraptions, the miles and miles of loneliness—had seemed so impossible then. Now, I can finally admit that at that time, I didn't think I would ever be able to *actually* finish. But after eight days on the trail—the packs, the gear, the contraptions, even the smells—it just is what it is. The longer I keep walking, the more this feels almost normal.

I'm out here, alone. I'm doing this.

As I lie here with my eyes closed, trying to fall asleep, I think about how that conversation with Mom up on the cliffs of Section 13 changed some things for me. Hearing Mom talk about what happened—or kind of *didn't* happen—with Dad makes me feel a little more willing to talk to him. Like I'm not hurting Mom by trying to figure out my relationship with Dad. I'm obviously never going to trust him the way I did when I was little, but maybe I don't have to quit on him altogether, the way he quit on Mom and the way he quit on our hike. Mom's right: We probably need to accept what happened and figure out how to forgive him at least a little bit, so we can move on.

I drape one arm over Murphy and can feel his ribs rising and falling beneath his layer of matted fur. Tomorrow, I'll get up and keep walking. Each day feels like a whole lot of painful baby steps in the grand scheme of this whole adventure, but at least I'm making progress.

<u>Day 8:</u> Section 13 to South Egge Lake
<u>Miles:</u> 8.5
<u>Total Trail Miles:</u> 64
<u>Day's Soundtrack:</u> James Bond theme song
<u>Injury/TP Count:</u> X

---

# CHAPTER TWENTY-ONE
# RUDE AWAKENING

The next morning, I'm dragged out of a dreamless sleep by the sound of loons singing. It's almost impossibly loud, to the point of actually being a little annoying. I've heard the eerie sound of a loon call on a lake before, but it's never been like this. The loons are *so* noisy on Egge Lake that it's entirely possible there could be, like, four hundred loons floating nearby. *How can such a small, peaceful-looking creature make that much noise?* I wonder, stuffing my head inside my sleeping bag for the night. It's a beautiful sound, sure, but it's also way too early to be awake.

Just as I finally start to drift off again, I hear something much less peaceful. I open my eyes and notice that, beside me, Murphy's head and neck fur are both lifted. The sound of rustling leaves makes its way to my ears, and I'm about 95 percent certain there is something *large* moving in brush nearby, somewhere away from the lake. It's up from my tent, in the direction of the main trail, I think.

Murphy begins to growl quietly.

There are a few possible options—it could be a massive squirrel, a raccoon, a porcupine, a deer, a fellow hiker. Or a bear. A massive squirrel or fellow hiker are the least likely—and also the least scary—possibilities.

I hear something that is obviously a wet, huffy snort, and know instantly that it's not squirrel or deer or human. It's some sort of beast. A large beast that snorts.

Are there wild pigs out here on the trail? Are wild pigs friendly, or are they fierce? I realize that *any* large, snorting animal that can survive out here on the trail, this deep in the woods, for weeks and years on end, is probably pretty tough and not a creature I'd like to cross paths with. Especially not when I'm alone.

Several branches crack noisily, and I realize it's probably not a porcupine or raccoon wandering around camp either.

I can't tell if anyone else in the other tents are awake yet. What am I supposed to do about the fact that there's a bear or beast or pig roaming around our campsite? Do I just sit inside my tent and wait this out, hoping whatever it is doesn't decide to eat me and Murphy for breakfast?

I rub my hand over Murphy's shoulders and ears, trying to keep him calm so that he doesn't start barking. What if he *does* start barking? Will that make us obvious targets?

There's a distinctive scratching sound coming from somewhere near where I tied up my bear bag last night. My life is obviously worth more than the meals in that sack, but if a bear gets all our food, we're sort of doomed. I'm already hungry, and it's not even full daylight yet.

I decide to risk taking a small peek outside, and slowly slide open the zipper of my tent—just a few inches, way down at the very bottom. There's a several-inch gap between the bottom of my rain fly and the ground, so I press my face against the floor of my tent and try to look out through that slim crack for a better view. At first, I can't see much—just a lot of leaves and sticks and the shimmery blue of my tent's rain fly covered in morning dew.

But then I catch movement, up the latrine trail and a bit past Julia and Maddie's tent. It's definitely not a porcupine, and I'm pretty sure it's not a raccoon, unless raccoons come in extra-mega-jumbo size out here on the Superior Hiking Trail.

"Bear," I whisper to Murphy, so quietly it's just my lips moving in the shape of words.

The creature's shaggy brown fur hangs in big, straight clumps off its belly, which drags strangely low to the ground. Its paws are huge, and its body is so massive that I don't understand how it's able to make its way through the forest without getting stuck between gnarled branches.

Murphy clearly knew it was a bear already, since his growl has continued since I first heard the scuffling outside. Luckily, he hasn't gotten any louder—it's just a low rumbling that I can *feel* more than *hear*, and the loons are so noisy that I hope the bear can't hear him at all. The last thing I want is for the bear to feel threatened and come after us.

The scratching sounds get louder, and then the bear's huffs and grunts intensify. It's not roaring, but there's something about its quiet little noises that are even creepier than a full-fledged growl. It's just taking its own sweet time, digging into our food bags, picking out the best bits to eat now and figuring out what to save for later. I chew my lower lip and rub Murphy's ears, trying to keep him calm so that *I* can stay calm.

Suddenly, I hear the desperate sound of a tent zipping open, and someone screams, "Get out of here! Shoo!" It's Angie. *Oh, Angie.*

Then John yelps, "Take the dairy! Take all of Angie's dairy! There's an Alfredo pasta that no one wants!"

Angie growls, then says, "You better hope this is the Charmin bear, bringing us a roll of toilet paper, John."

"Please don't eat them," I whisper quietly, hiding my face in Murphy's fur as I hug him against me. "Please, please, please don't eat them." I peek out of the tiny hole I zipped open in the door of my tent and see that Angie is now standing behind her tent—as if that's going to protect her from an eight-hundred-pound beast. Angie stomps her foot and growls at the bear, and I've got admit, I'm kind of impressed. It takes guts to stand up to a bear.

While I watch a slice of this action movie silently from the relative safety of my little tent (which, I'll note, could *easily* be sliced open by a bear's claws or stomped flat by one badly placed paw), Angie continues to scream at the bear until it finally lumbers off at a slow and relaxed pace.

"Are you freaking kidding me?" I hear Angie scream out a few minutes later.

"Is it safe to come out?" I ask, somewhat comforted by the fact that Murphy's neck hair is now flat and his growl has stopped.

"Are you okay?" Julia calls—to me or Angie, I don't know—from inside their tent.

"The bear is gone," John says, which is slightly more helpful than the words Angie chooses, which aren't exactly appropriate for polite company. "Along with all our food."

*Ugh.* This is going to be a very long morning. I don't even know where the nearest road is, so I have no clue how long we're going to have to hike before we have any chance of eating again. I'm glad we're all safe, but I can't believe a bear got all our food. I climb out of my tent, keeping Murphy's leash short and tight—just in case the bear is still nearby. And that's when I see it: my fancy bear-proof bag, tied tightly and securely to a tree, exactly as I left it last night. There are scratch marks on the tree, and prints in the ground nearby, but my food bag seems . . . totally fine?

"Did you hang your food bag last night?" Julia asks John and Angie.

"Yes," John says. "We tied ours on the tree next to hers." He points at me.

"Do you have a bear-proof food bag?" Maddie asks, looking somewhat uncomfortable. "Or was it just in a regular sack?"

Angie glares at her. "It's obviously not bear-proof, since a bear just took all our food."

"So . . . Why didn't you *hang* it high in a tree to keep it safe?" Julia asks, releasing her and Maddie's also-untouched food bag from the elaborate pulley system she'd used to string it up and out of a bear's reach the previous night.

"*Hers* was just tied to that tree," John blurts out, shooting me a look that tells me he blames me for what happened. "And her food isn't gone."

It soon becomes clear that John and Angie thought we knew something about this campsite that they didn't know. So when they saw Mom's fancy bear-proof bag just *tied* to a tree, rather than hung from a rope in a branch high off the ground like most people do to keep bears from smelling or stealing stuff, they figured they were safe following my lead. They clearly hadn't seen Maddie and Julia's food bag strung up in a high tree far away from camp. Which means they'd essentially set up a bear buffet and invited our furry friend to swing by and enjoy a picnic made up of the rest of their week's worth of food.

Now, foodless and frustrated, they have no choice but to backtrack to their car and get more food, less than twenty-four hours into their hike. I glance at Maddie and can tell she's thinking the same thing as me: This might be for the best.

Feeling bad for them, but also not *that* bad, I offer to help in the only way I can. "I'd be happy to give you the rest of the oatmeal in my food bag," I say. "I'd hate for you to have to pack up and hike out with empty bellies."

# CHAPTER TWENTY-TWO
# I'M AN ATHLETE, HEAR ME ROAR

We let John and Angie pack up and head out of camp ahead of us this morning, partly so we could help them get moving as quickly as possible, and partly so they'd go first and clear the morning cobwebs from the trail before we hike on. I didn't tell Julia and Maddie the second part of our strategy.

Once our little group finally sets out for the day, heading toward Crosby Manitou State Park, we stop after just a few miles so we can hike out to a little island between the two Sonju Lake campsites, where we pick a comfortable rock to sit for a snack and a rest. Murphy gets a chance to swim and chase water bugs while we relax, looking out over the pretty, hidden lake.

"I appreciate this Salted Nut Roll more than ever this morning," I tell Julia, who's enjoying a few handfuls of trail mix. "I wonder if John and Angie made it back to their car without killing each other. Think my goobery, plain oatmeal held them over?"

Julia shakes her head and shudders. "Can you imagine spending weeks out on the trail with either one of them? That is going to be a long hike."

"If they actually go through with it," I say.

"Truth," Julia says, laughing. "If a bear ate all my food on my first night out on the trail, I think I'd pick a different summer adventure."

If that had happened to me on day one, I *know* I'd pick a different summer adventure. Or . . . maybe I would have survived it and kept going. I don't really know for sure anymore. I have a feeling if I'd known about all the things we were actually going to have to deal with out here on the trail before we left home, I probably wouldn't have ever started this adventure in the first place. But I *did* start it, and here I am.

When we leave Lilly's Island and set out walking again, I notice that I'm feeling better than I have in days. Some of my soreness has melted away, and knowing we handled our second *major* bear encounter gives me added confidence. As we plod down the trail, Murphy's keen eyes help me notice dozens of bumpy toads hiding under leaves, and a snake that startles both of us as it slithers across the trail ahead of us. The day's miles are relatively easy, and our only real climb comes in the mile or so before we get to the road that will take us into the State Park.

We don't have to stop to collect or filter water all day, since we loaded up all our bottles at Egge Lake last night, and tonight we'll be staying next to Manitou River at a back-country state park site. There aren't any free Superior Hiking Trail campsites in the State Park, but Maddie got enough service on her cell phone when we brought Mom down from Section 13 that she was able to log in and book a park site on the night she knew we'd be coming through. It won't be like my and Mom's first night on trail, in Gooseberry Falls State Park campground, since there won't be flush toilets or drinking fountains or ice cream bars in our camp, but we might see a closed-door latrine as we go through the State Park parking lot—and at this point a closed door to pee behind sounds like true luxury to me.

As we wrap around the corner heading toward the final Superior Hiking Trail campsite before we'll cross into state-park land, something huge and black comes barreling toward us.

I scream and jump off the trail, worried my heart might thud right out of my chest and plop onto the dirt. Murphy, whose leash is attached to my waist today, yelps and snarls protectively. As soon as I'm able to reel him in and can take a second to process my surroundings, I realize the huge black creature is a dog. A very large, very loose, very curious dog.

"He's friendly!" a guy calls from somewhere up ahead. "Just scratch his ears and you'll be his new best friend."

I hear Julia muttering something about leashes and "some

people," and now I finally realize why the leash-always rule exists on trail. As friendly as this dog may be, having *anything* pop out and rush at you in the middle of the woods when you're not expecting it is terrifying. Especially for someone who shared their camp with a bear this very morning. And to add to the stress of it all, Murphy is still snarling, even though he usually likes everything and everyone and it's very clear this loose dog is no threat to him at all.

The guy heads toward us, snapping his fingers to get the dog to come. He finally clips a leash to the dog's collar and greets us. "Sorry about that. We haven't seen anyone else today, and Ike just loves to run."

"All dogs like to run," Julia says, her irritation obvious.

"Are you heading south?" Maddie asks the guy.

"Yep," he says, sipping water out of a long, bendy straw that's poking out of his backpack. "Just stopped to grab some water at the river to get me through the rest of the day. I've gone about nineteen so far today. Aiming for Egge Lake tonight, so I have another seven or eight to go. It's a short day."

"You're hiking almost thirty miles *today*?" I ask, horrified.

"I only have two weeks to get the whole trail done," the guy says. "So I'm making it work."

"How?" I gasp. "That's a lot of miles every day. There's no way a normal human can do that. My body would shut down."

The guy laughs and says, "During my military training, we used to do fifty-pound boulder carries for twelve miles in the middle of the summer, so this is nothing." He shrugs and adds, "Your body is usually capable of more than you think."

I'm sure he assumes hearing this story will motivate me or something. But to be totally honest, it just makes me glad I've never had to endure any kind of military training. I admire the people who are willing and able to serve their country, but I'm pretty sure I never will.

Maybe someday I *will* be able to carry a fifty-bound boulder for twelve miles or hike thirty miles in one day, but for now I'm just proud of myself for doing this. I don't really need this dude to motivate me, I realize; somehow, I've managed to motivate myself.

After we send the guy and his dog, Ike, off on their merry way, Maddie and Murphy and I hang back and wander slowly for a while as Julia huffs down the trail ahead at a quick clip. She's obviously still steaming about Ike being off his leash.

"I've never been athletic like that guy," I tell Maddie. "He's a whole other level of human."

From behind me, she says, "Define *not athletic*."

"Okay," I sigh, and try to figure out how to explain my sports history. "So, I played soccer with a couple friends from school until fourth grade, but as soon as I realized no one ever passed to me—like, I literally would go whole games without touching the ball—I knew it was time to quit. I tried gymnastics, but I kept falling and couldn't ever figure out how to wrap my body up nice and tight to do a somersault. And last year, when we had to take the a fitness test in gym class, I couldn't even do one *assisted* pull-up." I laugh, then add, "And then there was the time I fell off a treadmill when I went to the gym to try to work out with my dad."

Maddie laughs. "I'm sorry to hear about the treadmill. And it sucks that no one passed to you in soccer. Also, I can't do a somersault either. I'm not bendy enough."

"But you see what I mean, right?" I ask. "I'm not a sports person. I'm just not athletic."

Maddie whacks my arm with her hiking pole, so I stop and turn around. "*This* is athletic," she says as soon as I'm looking at her. "What you're doing? It's sports."

"Nah," I say. "This is just walking. I'm talking about stuff like swimming and soccer and basketball and football. I don't do that kind of thing."

She narrows her eyes at me. "Hiking is a sport. Being out here, carrying yourself from place to place on your own two feet? That's super athletic."

"Huh," I say, smiling just a little bit at this new information. "Well then, look at me. I'm an athlete." I flex my arms, the way I see some people do in pictures to make their biceps bulge, and am surprised to realize they actually *do* bulge a little bit. I don't think they ever have before. "Hey, I have muscles!"

"You are an athlete," she agrees. "Big time. You don't need to win some sort of trophy or do five back handsprings or conquer your fitness test in gym class to be 'sporty.'" She puts this in air quotes, then adds, "I'm gonna prove it to you by putting it in your language—you're a reader, right? Would you consider Katniss Everdeen to be athletic? Or that boss dwarf guy in *The Hobbit*? Do you ever see either of them working out on a treadmill or running through cones on a soccer field? No. They're out in nature, breathing fresh air, surviving. Right?" She cringes. "I haven't actually read either book, but I've seen enough stuff online to make a few guesses."

"Katniss won the Hunger Games," I scoff. "So *obviously* she's sporty. And if you're talking about Thorin, son of Thrain, son of Thror, King under the Mountain? Yeah, have you seen that guy work a sword or axe? It's insane."

Maddie laughs. "Both athletes, just like you."

"Yeah," I say, grinning a little more. I *am* an athlete. "You can call me the Hiking Megan Rapinoe! Or Backpacking Paige Bueckers! Or Serena Williams with trekking poles instead of a tennis racket! This is a game changer."

"I bet you never would have guessed I played Division One soccer in college," Maddie says, and she's right. I would not have guessed that.

"Is Division One the top level?" I ask. There's a reason I can only come up with a couple of the most famous athlete names off the top of my head—I'm not super familiar with the sports world.

"A few of my college teammates play in the National

178

Women's Soccer League now," she tells me. "That's the US pro league for women. I got injured and had to end my soccer career, but to tell you the truth, I enjoy being out here in nature more, and still feel like I'm in just as good of shape as I was when I was playing soccer four or five hours a day."

As we start to climb upward again, I feel my thighs, tight and strong. I'm an *athlete*. Who would have ever thought it possible? Not me, that's for sure.

Just as we start to come down the other side of the steepest uphill we've climbed so far today, I hear the sound of distant cars cutting through the quiet of the forest and realize we must be near the State Park entrance. I can't help but think about my mom and wonder if she's okay. We've gone fifteen more miles since we split from her, and I realize none of them have been even half as bad as the first five miles on day one of our hike.

My legs are strong now, my body feels capable, and I'm starting to *believe* I might finish this adventure. It's still sad to have to do it without Mom. She would have loved Egge Lake—the dragonflies, the colors of the sunset last night, and especially the noisy loons. Of course, the bear would have possibly killed her of a heart attack, but maybe if she'd been with us last night, the bear wouldn't have come at all. The thing I've come to realize is, each little change or choice can cause a dramatic shift in how the future plays out.

If Dad hadn't met Catherine that day at his office picnic,

he might never have decided to leave us and he might be on this trip with me today.

If Mom hadn't offered to go on the hike with me when Dad bailed, I might not have had the courage or space to ask her what had happened to break up their marriage and wouldn't have realized maybe it was time to consider forgiving him so we can move on.

If we hadn't had the strength to make it all the way to Bear Lake on the day we did, that night we were so tired of climbing and just wanted to quit, I might not have met Maddie and Julia and Murphy.

If Mom hadn't had to pee so early in the morning at Section 13, she might not have lost her balance and fallen.

If she hadn't fallen, I wouldn't have been forced to finish this trip alone.

If I weren't forced to be alone, I might never have begun to realize this is the kind of adventure I might actually be capable of surviving.

I hear tires on pavement up ahead. Since I studied the map carefully this morning, I know we must be nearing the road we need to cross to get to the entrance to the State Park. As we clamber down the final stretch of trail, I see something that almost makes me cry.

"Mom!" I yell, trundling forward as quickly as I can with Murphy attached to my front and my pack strapped to my back.

"Jojo!" she calls back, holding up her arms. I notice she's

not coming toward me, and when I look down, I see that she's wearing one of those cast-boot things. Running into her arms feels so good. It's like that feeling I get when I come home after a terrible day of school and see my mom waiting with a smile and a hug just because she can somehow sense my day didn't go so well.

"How did you—" I begin. "When did you—what are you doing here?"

Mom laughs, and that's when I notice Regina standing beside her car. Julia is already plunked down on the ground, eating a doughnut. A *doughnut*! And oh, beautiful day, there is a whole *box* of doughnuts yawning open on the ground beside her. And a pizza! Mom sees me looking at the pizza, and I have a feeling I might be drooling a little bit. "We've been here for a few hours, so the pizza will be cold. But we wanted to bring you a few things, and I wanted to see you and check how you're doing!" Mom says, her eyes sparkling with tears or happiness or maybe both.

"A few hours?" I ask, grabbing a slice of pizza from the box. It's cold, but soft, and the pepperoni is greasy and crisp and the first bite is absolute perfection. "Why?"

"We knew you were going to be camping at the State Park tonight, but we weren't sure how long it would take you to get here from your last site. And we didn't want to miss you when you went by, so we got here early," Mom explains. "We stopped along the way and got you some doughnuts and pizza, and *oh!*" Mom goes to the backseat of the car and pulls out a tattered copy of *Anne of Green Gables*, which is not a book I chose to put in any of our resupply boxes for the trip, but is suddenly exactly the book I want to read. "I figured you might be ready to trade books a little earlier than planned. We're going to meet you again in a couple days with more supplies and the next two books you had packed, but this might help hold you over until then."

I clutch Anne to my chest and think about the first time I read this story. Mom has always been a bigger reader, but this is one *Dad* read aloud to me. He'd never read it as a kid, and when Mom learned that, she insisted that he must. So, in third grade, Dad and I took turns reading chapters aloud to each other and we fell in love with Anne together. After Anne, we read *Pippi Longstocking*, and then *Heidi*, and then *Harriet the Spy*, some of Mom's other childhood favorites.

This feels like a kind of peace offering, for Mom to bring me *this* book, one that meant so much to me and Dad together. Like she's giving me her clear permission to bring him back into my life and start making new memories with him as a different kind of dad while still remembering all the things that made me love him before he left. "Thank you," I say.

Mom nods. "Oh, and we also brought you a whole buffet of new food to shop from so you can replace whatever stuff you're sick of. You can all pick and choose and fill your bags with enough new meals to get you through the next few days. Like I said, we'll meet up with you then, wherever you are along the trail, so you don't have to carry as much with you now."

Maddie rushes forward and gives both Mom and Regina a huge hug. "Doughnuts are my favorite," she exclaims.

While everyone finds a comfortable spot on the ground in the shade to sort through food bags and inhale some cold pizza, I rest my head on Mom's shoulder and wrap my arms around her middle. "Is it broken?" I ask.

"A small foot fracture," Mom tells me. "I get to wear this fancy boot for a while, and then I'll be good as new." She kisses my hair, and I'm tempted to remind her that I haven't washed it in ten days, but I guess she already knows that. And if she forgot, she'll certainly remember as soon as she gets a whiff of my head. "How are you holding up?" she murmurs into my hair.

"I'm still walking," I tell her.

"And you want to keep going?" she asks, pulling back so she can look me in the eye.

"I do," I say with a nod. "I'm going to finish."

"I never had any doubt," she says.

"Guess what else I'm finally going to finish?" I add. She gives me a curious look. After scrolling through pages and pages of books that Mom has downloaded on her e-reader, I finally picked one to read during our rests and evenings these past two days after she left the trail. Even though I've tried and failed to read it at least a dozen times before, this time I'm finally loving *Little Women*. "Can I just say how glad I am that you named me after Jo, not Amy, in that book? Because Amy . . . she's the worst."

<u>Day 9</u>: South Egge Lake to Manitou River
<u>Miles</u>: 10.5
<u>Total Trail Miles</u>: 74.5
<u>Day's Soundtrack</u>: Mockingjay whistle on repeat
<u>Highlight</u>: Seeing Mom! And getting a new book early! And cold pizza! <u>And</u> I got to pee in a closed-door latrine in the State Park parking lot!
<u>Important Note</u>: If anyone ever finds this trail journal, you can't ever spill this little secret: Mom and Regina gave us a lift down the mile-long stretch of paved road that led from where the trail popped out onto County Highway 6 to the spot where it started up again on the far side of the State Park parking lot. Since we still SAW that part of the "trail" (I don't count it as real trail if it's on paved roads!) as it whizzed by outside the car window, I'm counting that mile toward my total. But we didn't have to walk on a mile of boring pavement in the hot sun, and we got five lovely minutes in car A/C. Worth a weeny lie.

---

# CHAPTER TWENTY-THREE
# THE PLURAL OF MOOSE
# IS RUN

Yesterday, Mom warned us that there are storms in the fore-cast for the next few days, so we got up and started walking way earlier than normal today. Now we're finally almost out of the State Park, which means we've already gone more than half our planned miles for the day. And which also means I've been walking long enough to say that Crosby Manitou State Park is awful. It's pretty, sure, but it's also all thankless ups and downs and the views at the top of each climb are totally not worth it. I'm betting this is probably *someone's* favorite place on earth, but it's not mine and that's the simple truth.

The air is filled with fog, which has made our morning walk feel almost magical. There have been a few times today when I haven't been able to see more than ten feet in front of me. The whole world is draped in frothy white, making the trees look like giant trolls lurking in the mist.

There are stormy-looking clouds bubbling up at the edges of the sky, but the early-morning fog is finally starting to clear around us and it hasn't started to rain—yet. My legs feel strong and sure, and even though Manitou has been nothing but endless climbs and descents, I'm holding up okay.

I *am* looking forward to taking a long break sometime today, though, so I can get back to my book. *Little Women* is long—*really* long—but I'm charging through it fast and am finally almost done. I've been working on digging into this story for three years, off and on, so when I finally finish it's going to feel really good. If we get to camp early enough tonight, I should have time to read the end, and then I get to dig into *Anne of Green Gables*. That's reward enough to motivate me.

During this morning's first rest, I made the mistake of eating a caffeinated Clif Bar as a snack. I haven't really *felt* any different, except that I am a lot chattier than usual. Maddie says it's as if someone turned on a faucet in my mouth, and words just keep spilling out without any kind of filter or pause or off-switch. Julia is walking somewhere up ahead of us—she sometimes needs her space and quiet—and so for the past few miles, I've been recounting the plot of *Little Women* for Maddie, since she's never read it (and somehow hasn't seen *any* of the movie adaptations). She clearly won't ever need to read it now after my chapter-by-chapter replay.

I'm partway through telling her about icky-Amy's adventures in Paris when we decide we should stop to give

Murphy—and ourselves—a quick drink of water. (I will admit, Amy is slightly less annoying once she grows up a little bit.) Maddie and I stop in a spot where there are lots of trees overhead, but it's also a length of trail where we can see several hundred yards stretching out both ahead of and behind us. Most of the time, the Superior Hiking Trail twists through trees and rocks so it's hard to see where you've come from and where you're going. But this is one of the rare times when I can spin around and see the path stretched out in both directions, which is pretty cool.

While Murphy drinks, I take a sec to pop off my pack and grab a dried fruit bar out of my food sack. This is one of the new treats Mom added to our bags yesterday. She swears they taste better than boring and chewy dried apples, and she's right. It's not the same as fresh fruit (who would have guessed I'd actually be craving *fresh fruit*, of all things?), but it's better than eating more nuts. I'm totally nutted-out.

I'm still rambling about Amy and her maybe-romance-but-I-don't-want-to-spoil-it "friendship" with Laurie when I spot movement out of the corner of my eye.

There's something not-human walking behind us on the section of the path we just came through.

"Maddie," I whisper, pointing.

She follows my finger, and sucks in a breath. "Whoa," she breathes, pulling Murphy's leash in close.

It's a *moose* . . . but a moose in miniature. All long legs and bony ribs and no sign of the telltale antlers that I assumed all moose have. "I've never seen a real moose in real life," I say, watching as the animal quietly and carefully picks its way through the brush along the side of the trail. "My brother used to have a stuffed moose with super-big eyes and a soft tail that he slept with every night." I don't know why this story is spilling out, but I'm guessing it's still the caffeine. My mouth just doesn't want to quit. Maybe I should take up a coffee habit. My mom and I started watching *Gilmore Girls* together last year, and Rory Gilmore drinks a lot of coffee. She seems to be okay with it, and she's just a teenager. She's really smart, even. So maybe that's a sign that coffee is a good choice.

I continue rambling on. "I have a stuffed Sven the reindeer from the movie *Frozen*, which I guess I *thought* looked just like a moose, but now I'm realizing that reindeer and moose don't look at all the same."

"Jo," Maddie says very quietly, cinching her pack up. "We need to go. Right now."

"He doesn't look scary," I tell her. "Or she? Aren't moose friendly? Sven the reindeer is friendly."

"I don't know," she admits. "But I do know that you should never be near a mother moose and her child, and that right there?" She points at the small hornless critter sharing our trail. "*That* is a baby moose. And baby moose means we have to *go*, before its mom shows up and *forces* us out of here. I'm pretty sure an angry moose mom is as bad as a grumpy bear parent."

The caffeine kicks in again, and I snap my pack closed lickety-split. Maddie keeps Murphy's leash reeled in tight at her side. Very nearby, we hear a snort and at that terrifying sound, we both start to run. It's not a regular run, but more of a clumsy shuffle-skip as I dodge rocks and roots and try to keep myself upright. I hear the snort again and pick up my speed.

Out of curiosity, I glance back—and that's when I see a *massive* beast emerge from the woods onto the trail, just about ten feet behind us. It also has no antlers but is at least four times the size of the little moose, which tells me this must be Mama. She stands between us and her calf and then slowly, terrifyingly, turns her head to look at me. I am careful not to make eye contact but can't seem to look away. Even the bears I've seen along the trail seem small in comparison to a giant moose. It feels like she's towering over me, and I know that if she decided to charge—well, I'm not going to think about that.

The moose snorts again and I watch as it bends and then lifts one of its long front legs. To wave hello, or kick me, I'm not sure. But I'm guessing it's probably not just a friendly *hello*.

I turn and hoof it. I don't want to know what this moose has planned for me and have no intention of getting trampled to death by a not-so-friendly and not-so-cute version of Sven the reindeer.

I race after Maddie and Murphy, who are now a good forty or fifty feet up ahead of me. Even though I'm still fueled by caffeine, I don't dare talk again until we're at least a mile past the moose. And I don't have the guts to look back over my shoulder to check that we're not being followed until we've turned several sharp corners and the path behind us has melted into the forest again.

# CHAPTER TWENTY-FOUR
## SCOUT'S HONOR

After a full thirteen miles—my longest day on trail yet—we finally trundle up to our planned campsite. But as soon as we do, I am horrified to hear shouting and whooping and what sounds like dozens of voices. These are full-on Minnesota State Fair, busy water park, Six Flags-level *crowd* noises.

"Wow," Julia muses as we slowly wade into the campsite. "That's—"

She breaks off, and I finish what I'm pretty sure she was about to say. "A lot of boys?"

"It's a lot of boys," she agrees.

A man who I assume is some sort of group leader waves to us. "Howdy!" he calls out. "Just passing through?"

"Uh—" Maddie begins. It's late in the day, nearly six, and the next campsite down the trail is several miles farther along. Judging by our giant packs, the time, and the fact that I've already started to unload my tent and lay it out in the only flattish spot that's not already covered with someone else's tent, we are obviously not "just passing through."

"Looks like we're going to be bunkmates for tonight," Maddie finishes joyfully. "I'm Maddie."

The guy cocks his head and frowns. "So sorry, Marnie, but this site is already taken."

The three of us exchange a look. There is a very well-known trail etiquette that says sites along the Superior Hiking Trail can be neither reserved, nor declared "full." If a camper shows up and needs a place to crash, the right thing to do is to scooch over and make room for them—even if it's not ideal or easy, and even if it's the middle of the night. It's a trail *rule*, in fact. I'm guessing the rule exists so that no one is forced to push past their physical limits and walk farther than they're able to in a day. But sharing camp with strangers also leads to community and connections and has been one of my favorite things about our time out here. If we hadn't shared space at Bear Lake and met up with Julia and Maddie and Murphy, this whole adventure would likely have played out a lot differently for me.

"We should be able to find some space to set up. Just might need you all to squeeze in a bit closer to one another," Julia says frostily. I recognize this as *her* teacher voice, which makes me think of my mom and how she doesn't tolerate any funny business when she knows she's in the right. I can already pretty much guarantee Julia will win this battle.

"Well, ladies, I'm sorry to say that we were here first, and I've got a policy that my group doesn't share a campsite with strangers," the man says, making me feel a little less certain that Julia's going to get her way. "It's just our second night out here, and I made plans quite a few months ago to stop *here* for tonight—and we got here first today. First come, first served is how I see it. Apologies, but you'll have to keep on trekking down the trail and find another spot to snooze. Them's my rules."

Julia dumps her pack on the ground and says, "If *you* don't want to share, you might need to move along and find an empty site for yourselves."

By now, some of the campers or scouts, or whatever they are, have started to watch their leader bicker with us, and I hear one of them mutter under his breath, "I'm not walking another step tonight. If Gary makes us pack up and hike any farther, I'm out."

Looking at their collection of tired and miserable faces, I can't help but cringe. I'm guessing this group feels about as good as I did *my* second night on trail—which was *not* good. The boys look miserable, and I feel sorry for them—it's not *their* fault good ol' Gary has such a weird policy about not sharing campsites.

But that's when I realize it's also not *my* fault Gary has such a dumb policy. He chose to take his group out to hike on a trail where sites are supposed to be shared, and he doesn't get to change the rules just because that's what he's decided makes the most sense for him. More importantly, I realize, even if Gary *has* made up a rule of his own design, it doesn't mean we have to abide by it.

I'm sick of other people making decisions that impact me without getting a say in the matter. There's *no* reason this dude's dumb decision to try to claim a site for his group to camp in alone gets to ruin my night.

Just like there's no reason my dad's decision to walk out on his family gets to ruin my life or our relationship.

I'm sick of letting other people tell me what's going to happen, and then just rolling over and feeling sad and mad about it.

I'm sick of letting someone else's choices hurt me.

I'm sick of being told what I can or can't do, what I may or may not be capable of, and I'm not going to let it happen anymore.

"Sorry, Gary, looks like it's about time for you to adjust your policy," I blurt out, my voice sharp and strong. "We're not leaving, so how about we all introduce ourselves to each other and you all can stick around and consider us part of your group for the night? I promise I don't bite." I hold up my hand like a shield. "Scout's honor."

Gary glares at me, then scans Julia and Maddie—who are both now grinning. He scowls at Murphy, who wags his tail at the first sign of a stranger's attention. It's very clear our group does not pose a threat, and it's even *more* clear we're not going anywhere. Which means good ol' Gary's gonna have to figure out how to deal with us. I know all too well by now that, sometimes, figuring out how to accept the stuff you don't have any power over is the only way to get through life. Change is hard, but sometimes it's the only option you're given.

"If you expect a private site," Maddie says cheerfully, "I'd suggest booking a spot in a campground next time."

Gary grumbles as he wanders off. That's the last real interaction we have with their group that night, but it's not the end of them. Throughout the evening, we get to listen to them singing lewd songs, watch a whole lot of stick fights in and around the creek, hear tons of bickering and whining, and even eavesdrop on their not-so-smooth dinner prep. Let's just say Gary is *not* a happy camper when he discovers that the kid who was given responsibility for carrying the whole group's silverware forgot to pack it up at their last campsite.

Poor Gary might have a policy about sharing campsites, but I sure hope he doesn't have a policy about eating with his hands. If he does, group leader Gary hit a real losing streak tonight.

Day 10: Manitou River to Dyer's Creek
Miles: 13 (record for most one-day miles of the trip so far!)
Total Trail Miles: 87.5
Day's Soundtrack: "Under the Sea" (again)—thanks a lot, Mom. Your songs live on even though you're probably sitting around, eating waffles in bed, right now.

# CHAPTER TWENTY-FIVE
## ALONE, AGAIN

This morning, after we say a not-so-fond farewell to Gary and his group, we decide we're going to push hard and shoot for almost sixteen miles today—so that I can hopefully get all the way to Lutsen tomorrow afternoon. The weather forecast isn't looking good, and I'd rather not drag out the last few days in misery.

There are several campsite options scattered along the trail over the next six miles, but none of us really want to stop for the night after only six miles today—and the next campsite option *after* those is another full nine miles farther. Which means we have to hike six or sixteen today, and Maddie and Julia decide to let *me* choose how far to go. I pick sixteen.

I'd be excited I'm so close to finishing, but the trouble is, I've reached the point of this hike where I'm actually sort of tempted to give up *now*—out of a combination of exhaustion and flat-out boredom.

Each day of this hike has started to feel a lot like the last, and my legs—which *had* stopped screaming at the end of every day—started to ache bad again last night. I have two new blisters, one on each little toe, and my knee starts stabbing every time we stop to rest and I attempt to sit down. The ankle I twisted on the very first day has been clicking for the past twenty miles or so, and today when I woke up, it was a little swollen. I keep rolling it when I step funny on that side. It's as though my ankle is sick and tired of this trail and has decided to give up on its job of holding me up.

I've finally gotten used to the way I smell, and I've come to accept and choke down the food I'm stuck eating. But with acceptance comes boredom. I keep thinking: What's the point of continuing on all the way through my last planned mile when each vista is starting to feel a little bit too much like the last, and each step feels like drudgery?

Even though it's tempting to call Mom to come and pull me out *today*, I also know it would be ridiculous to quit here, when I'm so, so close to reaching the goal I set for myself. Just two more days, and I'll have done it. Two more days on trail, and I will have finished something I never would have thought was possible on my own. By tomorrow morning, I'll have made it farther than Dad and Jake. So even though I don't want to walk even *one* mile today, I'm going to shoot for sixteen to bring me that much closer to the finish line.

The morning's warm-up miles take us through a huge and gorgeous maple forest that is completely magical and somehow looks and feels like no other part of the trail we've come through yet. It's drizzling, which would be awful and miserable if it weren't so hot, but because it's still a thousand degrees, the gentle rain is a gift . . . even if it feels a little like sweat dripping off my face. I can hear low thunder rumbling far off in the distance, but for now we're still enjoying the calm before a storm.

Luckily, the pretty trees and morning birdsong help distract me from my blisters and sore knees, but unluckily, they don't make my legs hurt any less. When the rain stops after a few miles, we all agree we should take a long snack-and-reading break, at the top of something called Tower Overlook, gazing out at a hazy Lake Superior in the distance. During this stop, I finally get enough time to finish the last few pages of *Little Women*.

News flash: It was really good, and *might* even be worth a reread.

While we're sitting at this overlook, there's a wide enough view of the North Shore that it's easy to see just how many storm clouds are building along the edges of the big lake. So far, the storm that's been threatening us for the past two days hasn't arrived and the rain hasn't really been much of anything. I think we would all be happy just sitting on this giant rock for hours, since it's comfortable, breezy, and the perfect level of warm, but none of us want to get stuck in a downpour at the end of our longest day.

We walk along an easy trail beside a beautiful river for a

few miles, then head into Temperance River State Park. The waterfalls throughout this park are stunning, and when we reach the park's main area, we're able to get enough service on Maddie's phone that I get to text Mom a quick message to tell her I won't need another food and book resupply, since we'll be at the Lutsen gondola *tomorrow* (besides, I still have my copy of *Anne of Green Gables* to keep me busy).

As soon as I send the message, I realize I honestly can't believe that after nearly two weeks out here, it's almost time to return to normal life. One with endless water from a tap, hot showers, fresh food, unlimited toilet paper, and easy access to any book I'm in the mood to read. Even if Dad managed to destroy a whole lot about our life when he walked out, I'm suddenly realizing there's a whole lot left to be grateful for. And so many things that would have seemed totally impossible and crazy to me a few weeks or years ago now feel . . . almost normal.

When we pass by the long-awaited Mediocre Overlook later in the day, I'm ashamed to say I'm too lazy to walk the short spur trail out to see if it's as *meh* as promised. I guess I just don't have the energy for anything extra now, and I'm in full-on survival mode. I'm disappointed to miss it, but know that if I don't keep walking today, I'm not going to make it. I can almost guarantee I might collapse.

My feet hurt.

My knee hurts.

My ankle hurts.

My stomach hurts.

But the worst hurt is deeper down, from missing both my mom and dad.

By the time we start in on our last five brutal miles for the day, the clouds overhead look scary, almost like they've been tie-dyed with black and blue and white all swirled together. None of us discuss the weather that's obviously coming our way, but I can feel us all pick up our speed. We've been pretty quiet all day, but now we've stopped talking altogether. I just want to get to camp and get cuddled up inside my tent before any big rain hits.

We're marching down the trail from something called Carlton Peak when fat globs of rain finally begin to fall. At first, it's a relaxing patter. But in a matter of ten minutes, it turns into a full-on, drenching rain. Families who'd been out for a day hike to see pretty views are noisily scampering down the trail ahead of and behind us (except one little kid who is somehow carrying a full-size iPad on his hike and doesn't seem to be in any kind of hurry at all). Murphy looks like a giant wet rat, with his fur hanging limp and heavy against his body. I'm sure I look the same, but I'm more worried about the stuff in my pack than I am about the stuff on my body.

We stop just long enough to throw rain covers on our packs and then I put my head down, focusing on nothing except the trail at my feet. There are just a few miles left until we reach our campsite, and we don't have any choice but to get there tonight. The rain finally slows a bit as we pass through a parking lot that many day hikers use as their base point to climb up to the top of nearby peaks, but that lot is mostly empty now. Everyone sensible has gone home.

My blisters are rubbing inside my soaking wet shoes, and the wet rocks are making me slip and slide around—which isn't doing my knee any favors. I'm hungry, but my food is deep under my pack cover and I don't want to stop and dig it out, since I might lose Julia and Maddie in the process. My pants are now so wet that the bottoms of each leg are dragging in the dirt and I keep stepping on the cuffs. Worst of all, I have the song "Thunderstruck" by AC/DC stuck in my head, and it's not at all reassuring.

Luckily, the last mile or so to our campsite is easy hiking— flat, gentle, and filled with plenty of leafy trees that help block some of the fat raindrops from reaching the ground.

When we *finally* get to the Springdale Creek campsite, we're the only ones there.

Alone, again.

Julia gets to work right away, quickly setting up her and Maddie's tent, while Maddie offers to take Murph down to the creek to collect and filter enough water for all of us. I sit on one of the log benches some nice trail volunteer has installed around the campfire at this site, and drop my head into my hands. Sixteen miles is a lot.

"You okay?" Julia calls, from beside her tent.

"Yeah," I say.

"Want me to set up your tent for you?"

Though I *want* to say yes, I know the correct answer is no. I need to do this for myself. I'm so close to done, and I'm not helpless. If this adventure has shown me anything, it's that I can do so much more than I've ever given myself credit for. I'm kind of a beast. Maybe I'd actually do okay in the Hunger Games? Or at least maybe I could make it to the end on *Survivor*. I shake my head and start to pull the tent pieces out of my pack.

By the time Maddie and Murphy get back from the creek with our water bottles, the rain has started up again in earnest. The wind has also picked up, and the sky is dark like a bruise. It could be ten at night, considering how murky it is overhead. I drape my rain fly over my tent just as my three companions zip into their tent to change into dry clothes (except Murphy, who's stuck wearing his wet coat all night) and then call out to tell me they're going to lie down and rest for a while.

The wind is blowing even harder than it was when we first got to camp, and thunder rumbles around us in stereo. I'm guessing it's going to be a protein-bar-for-dinner kind of night.

I get my tent set up, but don't stake down the rain fly. A sudden need to pee forces me to run to the latrine before I can change into dry clothes or finish tying everything as securely as I'll need to in order to keep myself dry overnight. I leave my covered pack on the ground next to my tent, knowing I'll still need to get the inside of my little house set up and my food bag secured somewhere away from camp just as soon as I return from the toilet.

But when I get back to camp, my tent is not where I left it. Instead, it's blown halfway across the campsite and is pinned against a tree, upside down. "Come on," I mutter, softly to myself. Hot tears spring to my eyes, and it takes every ounce of self-control to keep from crumpling to the ground. "So much for being a Hunger Games champion."

Julia and Maddie are still both hiding out in their own tent and no other hikers are here with us, so I'm pretty sure no one saw my tent and rain fly tumbleweed across the campsite. Which means there's time to fix this dumb mistake before anyone else ever finds out what happened. But *I* know what happened, and that's bad enough. Eleven days into this one-hundred-plus-mile hike, and I just made a truly rookie mistake.

Sighing, I grab my assembled tent by one of the long poles that stretches across the top of the ceiling and attempt to drag it back across the muddy ground. My tent's not heavy (5.4 pounds *with* the rain fly, to be exact), but the task of tipping it upright and dragging it back into position in all this wind is clumsy and awkward and messy. As soon as I get it back to where it was originally set up, I hastily throw the rain cover back over the top, stake down the corners, and toss my stuff inside. Seconds later, the rain starts coming down even harder.

I jump inside and zip myself in. I'm totally alone, and for a few moments, I'm kind of glad. I'm not in a great mood tonight, and the thought of having to be friendly and grateful to Maddie and Julia makes me cringe. But when I start to strip off my wet and muddy clothes, there is a clap of thunder overhead that's so loud I actually feel the ground shake beneath me.

I zip open my rain fly and peek outside from the relative safety of my tent. I read in one of the hiking guidebooks that you're supposed to check the trees overhead for loose or broken branches just in case the wind gets so severe that they might be knocked loose and land on your tent in a storm. Death by falling branch is not something I have on my bucket list, so I scan the trees overhead to see if there are any murderous branches hidden within the pine trees. Luckily— or maybe unluckily, depending on how this storm shakes out—my tent is in a pretty open space, with no branches overhead at all. In fact, I'm totally exposed in this spot and now I'm worried about a lightning strike.

I wish my mom was here.

I've been thinking that a lot today. After seeing her yesterday, it made me miss her more. So much more. I know that's a little silly, since you'd think getting a chance to hug her and find out she's doing okay would help me to *not* miss her. But yesterday's surprise visit had the opposite effect. It reminded me how much I love spending nights along the trail tucked in beside her, feeling safe just because she's there. Like that baby moose, who had its mom nearby to make sure nothing bad could happen, I want my mom here to watch over me.

But instead, I'm alone. Totally alone. And I have no idea what's coming next.

That's one of the things that scares me most about being alone . . . the unknowing. That feeling of everything being okay in the moment, not realizing that just around the corner and just in the future, something awful could be headed my way. I felt fine in the moment just before Dad told me he'd left us, but now I know all too well that everything can shift in an instant. And once again, I have no one with me to hide behind or turn to or cry on.

At this point, I'd even be thrilled to have my *dad* here with me. Because I miss him, too. Not in the way I've missed him the past couple years: because he chose to walk out on us, because he chose someone else over me and Mom and Jake, because he broke life-as-I-always-knew-it, and because I miss how things used to be.

This missing is different; it feels real, and I finally, truly feel like maybe I'm ready to start over and move on. I want my dad back. I think I'm ready to accept what happened between him and my mom, and to try to forgive him for the choices he made. To see if maybe there's a way for us to move forward, together. He doesn't get to have the power to ruin *our* relationship, too.

The wind picks up again, whipping through the campsite

and whistling in the branches overhead and all around me. There's another crack of thunder, then I see a pulse of lightning fill the sky and light up the dark. I toss my wet stuff outside onto the muddy ground. The rain is pounding down even harder now, so I zip my tent the rest of the way closed and put on my dry nighttime clothes. I close my eyes and plug my fingers into my ears, trying to block out everything. But I can still hear the wind and, even worse, I can *feel* the rain and thunder. The ground is shaking and the sky is sobbing.

I start to cry, too. I'm trapped in this storm all alone, and all I can do is sit it out and wait. It's just like how I've felt these past few years. No matter how much I've tried to shut out the hurt and betrayal, it's still there. Even if I try to pretend everything is okay, the storm will still be raging all around me.

But it can't rage forever. I can handle it. I can survive any of this.

I open my eyes and breathe.

I've got this.

"You've got this," I say out loud. Then, quieter, but just loud enough for me to feel it deep down, "You've got this." I lie back on top of my sleeping bag and stare up at the blue roof of my tent, watching and listening and *believing* it's all going to be just fine, even as the storm continues to pound down around me.

<u>Day 11</u>: Dyer's Creek to Springdale Creek
<u>Miles</u>: 15.5
<u>Total Trail Miles</u>: 103
<u>Day's Soundtrack</u>: A little Lizzo and a lot of Thunderstruck

---

# CHAPTER TWENTY-SIX
# ENOUGH

I wake up on this last day of my hike to an unwelcome, steady drizzle.

While fat raindrops run down my face and seep inside my shirt and soak my hair, I shove all my filthy gear into stuff sacks wet, relieved that I won't have to pull any of it out again to use tonight. I might not bother *ever* unpacking this stuff, since I can't even imagine cleaning up the mess. It's gonna smell like a horse barn after sitting wet inside my pack all day. Or worse, like the inside of my brother's hockey bag at the *end* of a playoff season.

We all eat packaged bars for breakfast since none of us wants to stand around outside long enough to heat water or prepare anything else. At least I don't have to watch anyone slurping up globs of oatmeal.

About four miles after we set out for the day, the nonstop, drenching rain finally begins to slow. We decide to stop at the next campsite we pass to try to dry some of our stuff and grab a snack. As soon as we see one of the now-familiar wooden signs that always marks a campsite, I'm able to make out the lettering and see we're at Onion River. This is the very last site Dad and Jake slept in, before deciding to pop off trail the very next morning. Less than a mile farther down the trail, and I'll have passed them. This is where they quit.

But me? I'll keep walking. I'm just a little bit stronger; I know I can go just a little bit farther. Everything from here on out is new, an adventure for me alone.

After our snack and pee stop in the giant campsite, we head on and pass by the Onion River parking lot. The rain's back again now, but it doesn't even bother me anymore. Because I've made it. I conquered this whole adventure—almost half of it *alone*—and I did it all without Dad.

I'm strong enough.

I'm tough enough.

I'm fearless enough.

*I* am enough.

I don't even notice when the rain finally stops, not until the sun begins to peek through the clouds just as we reach Oberg Mountain. We come to a spur trail that leads up and around the top of the mountain that we've heard can't be missed, so we all drop our packs into the woods and climb up the extra trail without any gear. I feel freer than I have in months.

We have the top of the mountain all to ourselves, since the crummy weather has driven any possible day hikers to do other activities. But now, after this morning's downpour, the weather couldn't be more wonderful. The sun is shining, it's the perfect temperature, and even though my shoes are still wet, my blisters feel like nothing more than a memory.

From all way up here, Lake Superior looks like a giant blue jewel buried in a world of green. I can see for miles up and down the shoreline from the top of Oberg Mountain, and I vow to get Mom up to this spot just as soon as her ankle is well enough for her to hobble to the top. But until then, this is all mine. I earned it.

"You ready?" Maddie asks, standing above the spot where I've plunked down to take it all in. Murphy lies down beside me and drops his head on my thigh.

I glance up at her. "Do you think I could take some time by myself?"

She raises her eyebrows. "Uh . . ."

Julia strolls over and I add, "It's only a couple more miles to the Lutsen chalet spur trail, right?" I ask, pulling my damp map out of my pocket. I point to where we are and then run my finger across the map to show where we're headed. "Do you think we could meet up there, so I can try to do a few of my last miles alone?"

The two of them exchange a look. After a moment, Maddie shrugs. "We're all going the same direction, right?" Julia tilts her head to one side, questioning. Maddie says to her, "If she doesn't show up in a reasonable amount of time, we'll know she's somewhere between Lutsen and here, and we'll just head back and meet her . . ." She trails off.

"I just want to know I can do it," I add in a hurry. I've been thinking about this all morning—hiking alone, truly alone, is the only thing I haven't done out here. And it just feels like the way I need to finish this trail. By myself. "Please."

"Yeah." Julia takes a deep breath. "Okay."

Maddie grins at me. "Have fun! See you at the spur trail!"

Knowing they trust me enough to do this, that they believe I can handle it, gives me the extra burst of confidence I need.

Before I set out off the mountain after them, I take some time to sit and soak in the view. I let my eyes wander along the big lake's shoreline, wondering if I can see the spot where we started, but I know I probably can't. I'm more than one hundred miles away now. One *hundred* miles! It seems impossible that I've hiked that far. And even more unbelievable that I ever smelled clean.

I'm not sure how long I sit up at the top of Oberg Mountain, but when I finally stand, the rain is back. I've been staring out at the lake, scanning north to south, and when I spin around, I can see that another storm has built up inland behind me. The clouds are boiling and have bubbled up with more angry rain.

As I make my way around the top of the mountain path and head toward the short downhill trail that leads back to my gear waiting at the bottom, the wind kicks in. Without my pack on my back, I feel almost weightless. I double over to keep the gusts from blowing me off the edge of the cliff. By the time I press back into the cover of trees, fog has rolled in and the view that had been so vast and magical just a few minutes ago is now gone, wiped clean. The whole world is white. The lake is quickly erased from view altogether.

I keep walking.

Everything was so picture-perfect just a few minutes ago, and I'm not sure how it got so bad so fast. Just like how I'm not sure when my parents truly stopped loving each other. Or when Dad decided to stop trying. Everything seemed just right, and then, without any warning, it all turned ugly.

But I can't just sit here and wait and hope it goes away.

I've got to keep walking. There's no other way through this.

When I reach the spot where we dumped our packs in the woods by the main trail, the rain has morphed into a cold and steady mist. The fog is now thick enough that it has seeped down under the tree cover and is squeezing in on me from both sides of the trail. I tug my pack on and keep my eyes to the ground, careful of where I'm stepping.

As I walk, I realize I didn't have a clue what being truly alone out here would feel like. It's both unsettling and peaceful. Terrifying and exhilarating. A part of me hopes that Maddie and Julia will have stopped to wait for me somewhere along the way when they saw the storm building. I'm a little bit scared.

Maybe more than a *little bit* scared.

The mist has grown thicker, and I can only see a few feet in front of me now. I start scanning the trees I pass for a familiar blue blaze that marks my trail, but I don't see any. Sometimes along the Superior Hiking Trail they're infrequent; other times, it seems as if they're painted on every other tree. Today, I really wish whoever volunteered to paint the blazes on this part of the trail had been a *little* more spray-paint happy. I could *really* use a blue blaze right about now.

I stumble along, hoping I'm going the right way. The rain picks up, and the wind whistles around me. I can't hear any birds, the squirrels are silent, and all I *can* hear is the wind whining through the trees and my own breath huffing with each step. Each time I come around a corner, I look for Maddie and Julia and listen for the jingle-jangle of Murphy's collar.

My hiking poles *clink* noisily on rocks as I move faster and faster down the trail, and now that's another awful sound I can hear other than the rain and wind and my own panting. I slip, and my bad ankle gives out. My knee buckles under me and I start to fall. But before my pack can push me over and down, I scramble back to standing. The rain pounds at me, and my breathing grows faster. I know I'm walking much faster than I should be given the conditions.

I've been almost-running for several miles, I think, when I come to what I'm pretty sure is the spur trail that will lead to Lutsen's ski chalet on top of Moose Mountain. I'm pretty sure this is the trail I'm supposed to follow . . . but Maddie and Julia are nowhere to be seen. I call for Murphy, hoping to hear his familiar *woof* come from somewhere nearby, but I hear nothing. Just my own voice and the patter of rain and the hollow sound of pure silence.

*Alone.*

*Lost.*

*Lost and alone.*

"Hello?" I call, scanning the trail that leads off to the right that I am pretty sure I'm supposed to take. I don't have my cell phone—not that it would work way out here anyway—which means I don't have Mom's handy mapping app to check my position and find out exactly where I am. I dig into my pocket and pull out the paper map for today's hike, but it's completely soaked through. It almost melts in my hand. But even if I *had* a map, I have no idea how far I've gone past Oberg Mountain or where I'm currently standing on said map.

After yesterday's sixteen-mile hike, today's eight total miles should feel like nothing. I know I must be close to hitting that total by now. But even after almost two weeks out here, I'm still not good at guesstimating distances while I'm hiking.

*What if this is the wrong trail?* I don't ask it aloud since there's no one to hear me anyway.

No one can answer but me.

No one can fix this except me.

I spin in useless circles, looking at what I *think* is the main trail heading north, and then staring toward what I *think* is the spur trail that will lead a little farther east to where my mom is waiting for me at the end of this journey. My only option is to follow my instincts and the knowledge I've gained on this adventure—and hope I can trust myself.

So I turn right and trudge on.

Because of the rain, the trail is muddy and messy. I study the ground carefully, hoping I might see shoe prints that will help me figure out if Julia and Maddie are somewhere up ahead of me. But I find nothing. No sign that I've picked the right path.

Shortly after my turn off the main trail, I pass through a dense stretch of cedar forest, which feels *extra* dark in the rain and gloom. Part of me feels like I should be more scared . . . but for some reason, I'm not. Here I am, alone in the rain, it's dark and foggy, and I'm by myself in a place I've never been before—but I'm okay.

I'm doing this.

Before long, I come to a broad opening. I look around me, and even though it's foggy, I can tell this is a steep ski hill. The ground slopes up on my right and drops steeply to my left. In the summer, a ski hill looks weird—full of rocks and tiny trees and lumpy mounds where there should be smooth snow. But by getting to this hill, I know I *must* have taken the correct turn. I studied the map this morning and know I need to cross a couple of ski hills before I will reach the chalet, which is where the gondola to the bottom of the mountain departs from. The main Superior Hiking Trail wouldn't have passed over the ski hills, so I'm definitely on the right path.

I can't wait to see my mom. If everything goes as planned, she'll be waiting for me inside the chalet, and then we can ride the gondola down to the bottom of the mountain together. I'll finish this journey with her. I wonder if Maddie and Julia are up ahead of me; maybe they'll have met up with Mom already, and the three of them will be enjoying a plate of fries and relaxing together.

Mmmm . . . fries.

I can't wait to eat fries.

The ski chalet suddenly appears straight ahead of me, coming into focus through the fog like the moon rising over the horizon. At first, it's just a blurry outline, but as I step closer, it becomes clearer.

That's it.

The finish line.

I made it!

My face splits into a smile as I stumble down the walkway toward the chalet. The gondola is to my left, but I notice it's not moving. The big red bubble cars are just sitting there, stuck at the top. I make my way into the chalet, dropping my pack inside the door. I scan the giant room for my mom, eager to run into her arms and give her a huge hug. I am Katniss, returning home after my Hunger Games victory; Bilbo, returning home to the Shire after his quest.

But there is no Mom, no Maddie, no Julia, no Murphy. There's *no one* in the chalet except a few employees milling about, setting up tables with fancy white tablecloths and dishes.

"Is there a lady with a boot in here somewhere?" I ask the nearest employee. He looks at me like I'm crazy. "She has a bad ankle," I explain, pointing at my own leg. "She would have ridden the gondola up?"

"Gondola's not running," the guy says. "Weather's too bad. When the wind gets over fifty miles an hour or if we have storms, gotta shut it down." He grins at me. "You hike in?"

"Yeah," I say, feeling the disappointment like a punch in the belly. "I just finished one hundred and eleven miles. I was supposed to meet my mom here so we could ride down the mountain together."

The guy shakes his head. "You might be walking a few more miles to get down. Unless the weather clears, no gondola today. We have a wedding reception up here tonight, and the guests were all planning to ride up in the gondola. They'll probably have to come up on four-wheelers instead. Bummer."

Bummer, indeed.

"Did you see two other women come in a little bit ago, with a big shaggy dog?" I ask. "They would have had packs, too."

"No dogs allowed in the chalet," the guy tells me, setting forks to the left of the plates he's just distributed on tables. "But you can check out the deck if you want." He points through the big glass windows, to the wraparound deck that surrounds the ski chalet on three sides. Even with the fog, I can see that there's no one out there. But I can't see anything

**217**

beyond that. "Hey, we have a couple burgers and a few orders of fries ready in the window that aren't going to get eaten. You can take whatever you want—on us. Grab a soda if you want; I won't tell anyone."

I look at the little grill area and see two foil-wrapped burgers sitting under a warmer, alone in the self-serve window. There's an order of fries perched beside them. The soda machine has an ice dispenser and lemonade. "You don't need to tell me twice."

I swipe all the food, grab a drink, and make my way outside to the deck to wait. For what, I don't know.

This feels too familiar. I close my eyes for a second and suddenly, I'm back in my living room, waiting for my dad to come and get me for our pizza dinner. The night our lives fell apart. Me, just sitting there alone, waiting for someone who won't ever come. *But this is different*, I tell myself as I slather ketchup all over the bun of my lukewarm burger. It's different, because this time, I know pretty much anything is survivable. I'm all alone, and it's not awful.

I don't know how I hiked 111 miles.

But I did.

Before Dad left, before all this, I didn't know what I was capable of surviving. I always *hoped* I could handle pretty much anything. But until you actually go through something like this, you don't really *know*. But now, I do know.

"Jo!" I've just unwrapped my second burger and taken a

massive bite when I hear someone yell my name. I turn, and there's Maddie, with Murphy working hard to tug the leash off her waistband. She unclasps him and he scrambles as quickly as he can over the metal decking to reach me. "Oh my gosh, you're here." She turns over her shoulder and screams, "Julia, she *is* here!"

"Jojo." I turn as I hear someone call my name from the other side of the chalet deck. I spin around and there's *Mom*. "You made it!"

I toss the rest of my second burger to Murphy and jump out of my chair. I run to my mom and wrap her in a tight hug. "I made it," I confirm. "And I didn't even die. Or get eaten by a bear, but we did *see* one. Two, actually. And a moose and its baby! And I slept alone in my tent and set it up by myself and . . . Wait, how did you get up to the top of the mountain? You didn't *walk*, did you?"

She laughs. "The guy down at the bottom of the gondola, he felt bad for me after I gave him a whole sob story. I explained that I was supposed to be up here meeting you to celebrate you reaching the end, and I pulled the pity-me card with my ankle boot and told him *how* I hurt it, and after he finished laughing at me for falling on a latrine trail, he offered to get me a lift up the ski hill in one of the maintenance vehicles."

Julia careens around the other side of the chalet then and blurts out, "Oh, Jo, I'm *so* sorry. With all the rain and the fog that rolled in, we somehow missed the turn for the spur trail and when we realized we'd passed the spot where we were supposed to meet up with you, we raced back and waited, but you must have already passed and—" She cuts herself off and her eyes go wide when she realizes Mom is standing beside me. "I'm so sorry, Mrs. Conlan. I swear we took good care of her this whole time she was with us, but today—"

"Oh boy," I mutter. "She used your teacher-name."

"It's fine," Mom reassures both Julia and Maddie. "Jo's obviously fine. I'm sure you took great care of her, but this girl is also perfectly capable of taking good care of herself." She rests her chin on top of my head and squeezes me again. "I love seeing you, but I've got to be totally honest—you don't smell great."

"Wait until I take my shoes off . . ." I warn.

Since the rain has almost entirely tapered off now, I offer to hang out outside with Murphy while Mom, Julia, and Maddie go inside to charge electronics and fill their food bag with all the new stuff Mom has brought up the mountain with her. She's got enough food that they should be able to make it the rest of the way to the northern end of the trail without having to stop to resupply again. In a week or so, Mom and I are going to drive up to the Canadian border, pick them up, and return them to their car parked way down by the start of the trail on the Wisconsin border. I'm excited we'll get to help them celebrate the end of *their* journey.

Murphy and I chill out, sharing the sleeve of fries. I slurp my lemonade and even when he gives me the saddest puppy-dog eyes ever, I don't share *that* with him. But I do get him a bowl full of water from inside, and I even drop in an ice cube so he has something fun to play with while he drinks.

Once Julia and Maddie have sorted all their old and new stuff, hit the *indoor* bathrooms, and refilled their water bottles with fresh water from the chalet, it's time for my partners to ditch me and hit the trail again. "We have a few more miles left to walk before we get to our campsite for tonight," Maddie says sadly. She gives me a huge hug. "Love you."

"Love you, too," I tell her. I wrap Julia in a hug and say, "I'm really going to miss you guys. Good luck with your last seventy-five miles!" As I say that, I shudder—I'm glad *I* don't have another seventy-five miles to walk this week. Maybe next summer I can try to conquer some more of the trail, but 111 miles is enough for me now. I bend down and squeeze Murphy. I don't say it out loud, but I'm going to miss him most of all.

As they start to walk away from me, Murphy holds back. He pulls against his leash, trying to stay with me. It gives me a little thrill to think the big guy maybe likes me best. Or maybe he just likes that I shared my fries and burger. "See you soon, bub," I tell him, ruffling his shaggy fur.

Just as they turn the corner to walk down the path that will lead them back into the woods, the guy I talked to earlier pops his head out of the chalet and says, "Hey, the winds died down just enough that they're letting the wedding party ride the gondola up now. If you want to hop in one of the cars as it goes down, you're welcome to. But you better make it quick, since I don't know how long they're going to keep things running."

Mom and I rush inside for my pack, then make our way out to the gondola boarding area. We jump into a car just before its doors slide shut and I collapse against the seat facing forward. Mom slides down next to me and even though I smell and am sweaty and soaking wet from the rain, she pulls me against her and holds me tight.

From inside the glass-encased bubble, I can't see much—fog has completely obscured the view of Lake Superior that I'm pretty sure should be visible from the gondola window. The wind tugs and pulls at our pod—which is hanging from the pulley system by one measly-looking little hook—and the car sways and shakes like a leaf on a tree in a storm. But we're safe and out of the rain and we're on our way home—together.

Since I can't see anything on the ride down the mountain anyway, I close my eyes and nuzzle against my mom. We each lean into each other. "You did it," she says.

"*We* did it," I counter. I look up at her and smile. "*And*, by the way, I finished *Little Women*."

"Did you?" Mom asks, sounding surprised. "Did you forgive Amy by the end? Can you look past all the annoying stuff she did and find a little room to like her . . . even a little bit?"

"I'm working on it," I say, knowing we're probably kind of talking about both a book character *and* my dad. I am working on forgiving him, too, and am planning to set up a pizza date sometime this week, so we can talk through a bunch of stuff—and so I can brag about beating him on my hike. "I'm still glad you named me after Jo. She's the best."

Mom hugs me tighter and whispers, "I agree. Jo *is* the best."

The gondola slows to a stop at the bottom of the mountain, and I groan as I stand up. I grab my pack off the ground for the last time, hooking the straps over my shoulders as we stumble toward Mom's car. I wrap my hand around Mom's arm and pretend to help her through the parking lot. But the truth is, I'm leaning on her just as much as she's leaning on me. Even though I now know I don't *need* her right beside me, it's still nice to know she's there. We've got this.

Maybe I started this journey because I wanted to prove something to Dad.

Maybe I set out on this adventure to show both me and Mom that we could do it, that we can survive on our own.

Maybe those are the reasons I started . . . but I finished it for *me*.

<u>Day 12</u>: Springdale Creek to the Lutsen Gondola
<u>Miles</u>: 8
<u>Total Trail Miles</u>: 111—DONE!

# AUTHOR'S NOTE

Preparing to write this book took a tremendous amount of firsthand research, but it was the most enjoyable and rewarding research I have ever done for a story. I wanted the setting and emotions of Jo's hike in *Just Keep Walking* to feel as accurate and impactful as possible, which meant I knew I'd need to live through a similar trail experience if I wanted to get things right. And so, after months of Superior Hiking Trail research and trip planning from afar (while I was outlining and writing and planning bits and pieces of this story), my then-thirteen-year-old son and I set off on the exact journey I set up for Jo and her mom in the book—one hundred-ish miles, over the course of twelve extremely challenging days, wearing the same stinky outfit for almost two weeks in a row.

Our goal, just like Jo's, was to hike together from Castle Danger to Lutsen along Lake Superior's North Shore, with one planned "Zero Day" (a day where we sat around watching TV in a motel room, eating ice cream, and sleeping in a real bed) to keep us from quitting. We faced dozens of setbacks, including a whole carload of stolen gear, a bear encounter, plenty of minor injuries, a significant lack of water (due to a summer drought), haze and smoke from

nearby forest fires, and total exhaustion.

I chose my son to join me on the adventure, in part because he was the only kid in my family who was willing to go, but also because he's a total hoot, chats a lot, has a great attitude, and is extremely helpful and encouraging when it comes to adventures like these. A lot of Jo's personality traits were inspired by my son's observations and comments on the trail, and his humor and company definitely kept me going many times when I wanted to quit.

We didn't end up making it all the way to our end-goal of Lutsen (heat, forest fire-related trail closures, desperately missing our dogs and the rest of the family, and two bad knees for Henry forced an early exit), but we did make it ninety-nine miles and I was able to finish hiking the last leg of Jo's planned journey on a later trip, so I could map out the last section of this hike to ensure I had the setting exactly right for every day of this novel.

Growing up in Minnesota, I have spent much of my life surrounded by nature. I've always enjoyed relaxing walks in the woods (the flattish kind), I usually like sleeping in a tent (if I have enough padding under me, and the weather and bug conditions are *just right*), and I love paddling a canoe or kayak on the lake, surrounded by loon calls and the gentle lapping of waves. But I've never been much of a hiker. My husband and I attempted to hike a section of the Appalachian Trail after college, before we moved to the wilds of New York City and figured we'd be leaving all traces of nature behind us for a long time. We made it about one hundred miles on that trek, but I absolutely *hated* the hike, and vowed to never do anything like it again.

Then, twenty years later, I found myself planning yet another hike along the edge of my beloved Lake

 Superior—this time, as research for a book and as an excuse for extended quality time with my teenage son. Over the course of the two summers after that first one-hundred-mile adventure with Henry, I ended up finishing the rest of the Superior Hiking Trail in bits and pieces, and I even spent a few nights out on the trail on my own . . . alone (which was, admittedly, one of my own greatest fears). And I survived.

I'm so glad I gave hiking another go, and I'm thrilled Jo's story forced me to get back out and enjoy some quality—and yeah, also sometimes torturous—time on the trail. Because hiking suits me. The quiet and tranquility of nature, breathtaking views, endless space for creative thinking, hours to sit and read in a tiny chair each night, and so much exercise that I can easily justify a daily candy bar or two. Life doesn't get much better than that!

If you would like to learn more about the Superior Hiking Trail, or would like to become a member or research an adventure like this of your own, visit superiorhiking.org. I would encourage everyone to attempt a journey like this at some point in your life—whether it's large (many days, like Jo) or small (maybe just an hour or two)—to enjoy the beautiful nature that surrounds us in our busy lives.

We're so lucky previous generations had the foresight to set aside many portions of our earth to preserve as wild areas—whether those natural wonders are as urban as Central Park in New York City, or as remote as the Boundary Waters Canoe Area Wilderness in Northern Minnesota. Be sure you take some time to get out and explore the wild world and do your part to help preserve it for future generations. And if you *do* attempt a journey like this, please make sure you reach out and tell me all about it (and maybe consider writing about your own adventure!)! I can be reached through my website at erinsoderberg.com.

Ten percent of the proceeds of this book will be donated to the Superior Hiking Trail to help support its management and maintenance for future generations of hikers.

# APPENDIX

**Latrine:** An open-air toilet found in each of the campsites along the Superior Hiking Trail.

**Blaze:** The blue rectangles painted on trees or rocks that help hikers stay their course on the trail. (Note: That cute hat is a bug net.)

**Spur trail:** A side trail that goes *off* the main Superior Hiking Trail and often leads to pretty views or other points of interest. Note: Adds extra miles to the day's planned hike!

**Campsite:** These are official spots to stop and sleep for the night that are built by volunteers who help create a fire pit, maintain the latrine, and make nights comfortable for those who are sleeping under the stars. (Thank you, volunteers!!)

**Water filter:** Drinking water straight from a stream, lake, river, or pond is dangerous, as there could be bacteria in the water that might make you very sick. Henry and I used a squeezable water filter on our hike, but some people use other types of filters or iodine tablets to clean their water before drinking.

**Camp chair:** A tiny, fold-up chair that makes nights and rest stops much more comfortable! Weighs about a pound, but I think it's worth every ounce of its weight.

**Backpack:** This is everything I carry in my pack for a few nights out on the trail (I have published a full list of what's included in this picture on my website, if you want to see the contents listed out in greater detail!).

**Scat:** Animal poop (left by bear, moose, wolf, deer, etc. I'm pretty sure these giant pellets are moose scat!)

**Beaver pond:** A still pond or lake that is created when a beaver builds a dam or lodge that stops a river from flowing.

**Boardwalk:** A man-made walkway that keeps your shoes dry—and helps protect the trail—in boggy, marshy, or wet areas.

**Gondola:** A bubble-like enclosure that carries people straight up and down a mountain on a swinging pulley-like system. (Note: Because I am afraid of heights, gondolas *terrify* me— but it was better than hiking a few more miles to get to the bottom!)

# ACKNOWLEDGMENTS

The most important thank-you for this book obviously goes to my son, Henry. After his backpacking camp was canceled a few summers back, because of COVID restrictions, I didn't want him to miss out on the opportunity to explore the woods—so I offered to take him on a hiking trip myself, even though doing so was very much *not* within my comfort zone. Slowly, what started as a simple plan to go on a small backpacking adventure together turned into a book idea . . . a book idea that shifted our casual camping adventure into a one-hundred-mile hike over the course of two weeks. We researched, we planned, we pretended to train, we shopped for food and gathered supplies, and then we set out into the woods without any real idea of what we were getting ourselves into. But Henry kept a positive attitude (mostly) and somehow filled all those long trail hours with enough fun stories and one-liners that we were able to keep walking.

Thanks also to my incredible friends (and neighbors), Kassy Miller and Regan Hartney (both of whom also happen to be wonderful middle school teachers!), who offered to join me for the final fifty miles of the Superior Hiking Trail, a stretch between Grand Marais, MN, and the Canadian border. Even though neither of them had any prior backpacking experience, they were both willing and eager to give it a go. Thank you for keeping me laughing literally *all day long* for fifty very hard miles. Kass, remember that day you "almost died"? I'm glad we all made it home to tell the tale and tease you forevermore.

Finishing the full three hundred-plus miles of the Superior Hiking Trail wouldn't have been possible without lots of rides, resupply boxes, meals, company, moral support, and help on the home front from:

- My parents, Kurt and Barb Soderberg, who delivered food resupplies and ice cream to various trailheads during my and Henry's adventure, and also dropped me off at a lonely trailhead one rainy morning when it came time for me to set out on my own for a few days. Camping alone certainly isn't my favorite thing, but I survived!

- My in-laws, Peggy and Steve Downing, who shuttled us out to the Castle Danger trailhead that very first day (when we had no idea what we'd signed up for) and fed us many meals on our way to and from the North Shore.

- My husband, Greg, who took on all kid and dog duties while I was off exploring the woods, and who also kept me company on a long birthday weekend hike to tick off even more beautiful trail miles surrounded by fall colors.

- My two amazing daughters, Milla and Ruby, who have

listened to endless stories about my trail adventures and let me disappear into this story for weeks at a time. I'm excited to take you both out on my favorite Superior Hiking Trail sections (for much *shorter* trips than Henry got stuck doing with me, I promise!).

- My mom, Barb, and our family friend, Jill Anderson, who picked us up at Crosby Manitou State Park and took us out for a meal at a fancy restaurant on Lake Superior before returning us to the trail, full and rested.

- The families on my daughter Ruby's soccer team, who all chipped in for an REI gift card after our full packs were stolen out of the back of the car one night, right before we were set to leave for our trail adventure. Your generosity during a really frustrating event was so appreciated and made me even more determined to keep walking when things got rough.

- All the great people we met out on the trail, but especially Tom and Dan, who spent two trail nights in a row with Henry and me—at Bear Lake and Kennedy Creek—and gave us the support, company, and supply of fresh water we needed to not give up after a really hard stretch—even though we really, really wanted to quit and go home.

As always, I am so grateful to my top-notch publishing team: my brilliant and wise dream of an editor, Sam Palazzi; my supportive and smart agent, Michael Bourret; cover illustrator Oriol Vidal, who has once again managed to capture the heart of my story in his stunning art; and the whole Scholastic team that I absolutely LOVE working with and feel so lucky to have on my side: David Levithan, Ellie Berger, the whole Book Fairs and Book Clubs team, Production, Design, Publicity, Marketing, Sales. I am so lucky to have you all on my team. Thank you for everything you do to support my books but also to help kids everywhere find great stories and cultivate a love of reading for fun.

Finally, thank you *thank you* to the Superior Hiking Trail volunteers, employees, explorers, and supporters—who have created and maintained this incredible trail and fostered a supportive trail community that lets city-people like me slip away into the woods for a while.

ERIN SODERBERG DOWNING

# CONTROLLED BURN

## ONE FIRE DESTROYED HER LIFE.
## CAN ANOTHER SAVE IT?

"A gorgeous, tender,
wonderful book. *Controlled Burn*
is a testament to the power
and beauty of everyday moments
of bravery, compassion, and love."

**—ANNE URSU,** AUTHOR OF *THE
TROUBLED GIRLS OF DRAGOMIR ACADEMY*

**■SCHOLASTIC**

# CHAPTER ONE

I felt the fire before I saw it. It wasn't the suffocating heat or the smell of smoke that hit me first. Nor did I see the claws of flames that eventually reached into every corner to rip apart our lives. It's hard to explain what it means to *feel* a fire without sensing the heat of it, but that's what it was—a feeling. Maybe I noticed a change in the air, or got a weird Spidey-Sense that something was wrong? I guess I'll never know for sure.

All I *do* know for sure is, I was sitting on the couch, listening to music and thumbing through Instagram, when our house caught fire. Scrolling through my feed, I saw that a kid from my Spanish class had gotten a super-cute corgi puppy. A couple of people's stories had just reminded me it was my friend Isabel's thirteenth birthday (I quick-posted a happy-birthday message, along with an old pic of the two of us from fifth-grade field day, plus hearts and a bunch of smiley faces). I'd also learned that a bunch of girls (a group I'm only sorta friends with) were out bowling together, which kind of made me jealous. A few minutes earlier, my mom had posted her Mom version of an artsy Insta picture—a glass of red wine perched beside a bright green plate loaded with grapes and cheese, all sitting atop a paperback copy of some book with a bunch of flowers on the cover.

Both my parents were out; Mom was at her book club across the street, and Dad was working at the hospital. The only things I'd been tasked with were tucking my sister,

Amelia, in, convincing her to fall asleep (not the easiest job), and unloading the dishwasher. A pretty regular kind of night.

I don't know what made me pull out my headphones, but I did—and that's when I felt it. A tingling, this *feeling* that something was not quite right. I slid my phone into the front pocket of my hoodie and pulled a blanket up over my knees, listening for creaks and voices. I won't lie; I was tempted to wake my little sister, so I'd have someone to comfort me. Even though she's younger, Amelia is the brave one, and she could always figure out how to make me laugh. In times of danger, I'd much rather hide under my covers and come out when everything is marked "all clear." Besides, I've half watched enough scary movies at sleepovers to know that having a *feeling* something isn't quite right means something probably *isn't* right.

Pretty much every possible scenario passed through my head. A sudden tornado. A nest of killer spiders. An intruder lurking around the corner in the kitchen, waiting to jump out and get me. All those things terrified me, and all of them suddenly seemed very possible.

Our basement had been ripped apart for months—we were finally getting a second bathroom, and a family room with a TV and hopefully a little fridge that would have cans of soda and bottles of Gatorade. (Dad was mostly excited because we were also getting a fancy new electrical panel that would let us run the toaster *and* the coffeepot at the same time without blowing a fuse.) Just this past week, some of the guys who were working on the project had dug a big